# *The* BILLIONAIRE'S UNEXPECTED BABY

*winning the billionaire series*

# *The* BILLIONAIRE'S UNEXPECTED BABY

*winning the billionaire series*

Kira Archer

Entangled Publishing, LLC
2614 South Timberline Road
Suite 105, PMB 159
Fort Collins, CO 80525
Visit our website at www.entangledpublishing.com.

Indulgence is an imprint of Entangled Publishing, LLC.

Edited by Alethea Spiridon
Cover design by Fiona Jayde
Cover art from iStock

Manufactured in the United States of America

First Edition January 2018

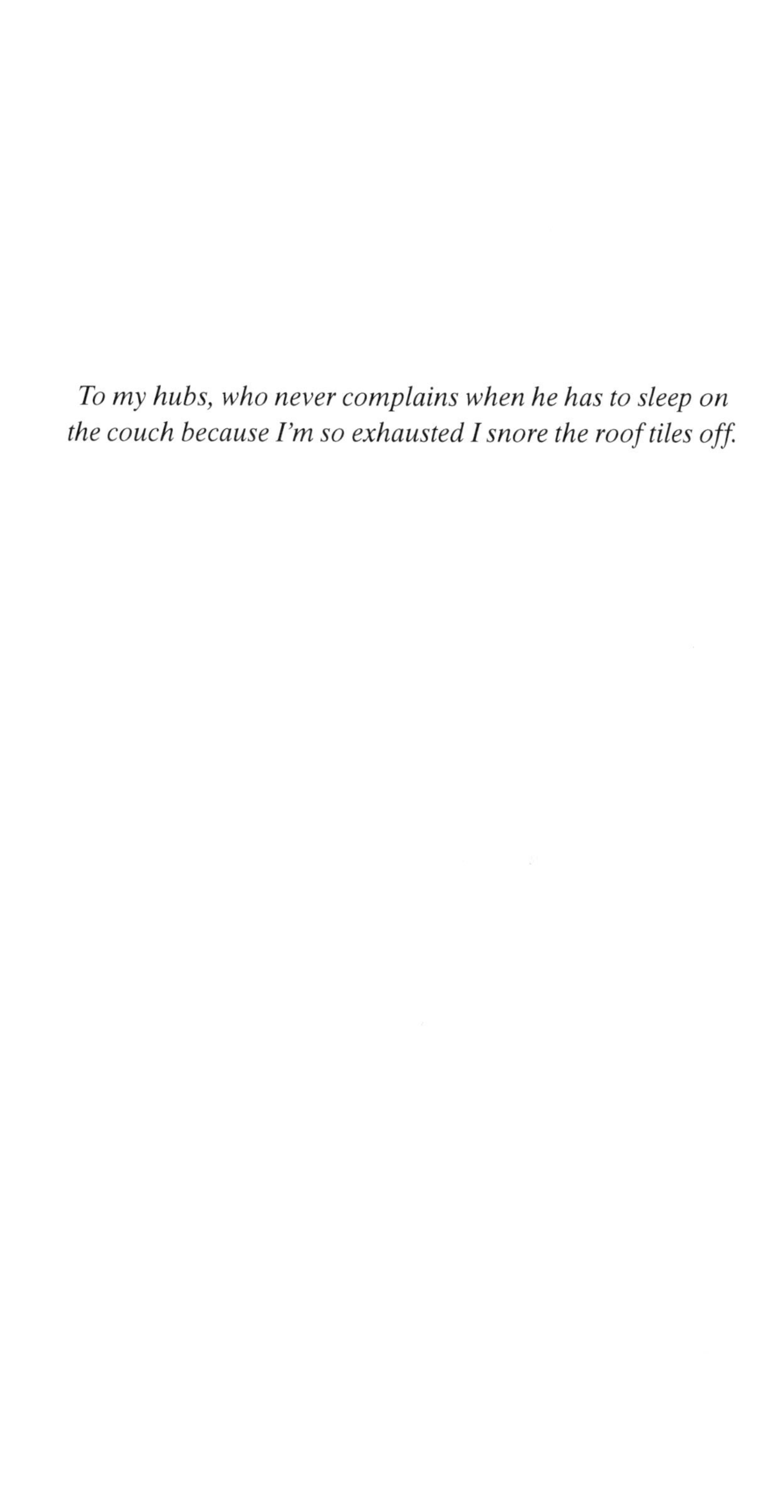

*To my hubs, who never complains when he has to sleep on the couch because I'm so exhausted I snore the roof tiles off.*

# Chapter One

Brooks Larson was the luckiest SOB on the planet and he knew it.

He leaned against the railing of his yacht, took a large sip of ridiculously expensive champagne, and a deep breath of crisp ocean air.

"Enjoying yourself?"

Cole Harrington, Brooks's partner and best friend since college, joined him at the railing.

"Hell, yes. We just closed one of the biggest deals of our career, making us disgustingly wealthy—"

"Which we already were," Cole said.

Brooks ignored that. "And I'm floating around in this magnificent tub of luxury surrounded by gorgeous women. Is there anything better in this world?"

"Yes," Cole said with a smile that made his friend's heart clench.

Brooks followed Cole's gaze to where Kiersten and Piper, Cole's wife and baby daughter, were lounging in the shade on a chaise longue.

"Are you really happy?" Brooks asked.

Cole scowled at him, but Brooks shook his head. "No. I'm not being sarcastic or trying to be insulting. I really want to know. You're married. You have a baby. You've promised to be with the same woman for the rest of your life and have produced a tiny, crying little human who has effectively trapped you into adult responsibility. Don't you miss being... free? Having your own life?"

Cole snorted. "Nice way to describe my family. And your goddaughter. And yes, to answer your question, I really am happy. And no, I don't miss being free. I *am* free. I *do* have my own life. My life is there," he said, pointing to his wife and daughter. "Everything I ever wanted is right there. I just never knew it until I met her."

Kiersten looked up at that moment and smiled at her husband and, for a brief second, a small twinge of what might have been jealousy wormed its way through Brooks. What would it be like to have someone look at him the way Kiersten looked at Cole?

He shook his head and pushed the thought to the back of his mind. No one would ever look at him that way, and he sure as hell never wanted anyone to.

"Well, I'm happy for you, but you keep all that monogamy over on your side of the boat. I'm happy playing in the singles pool. Speaking of which..." He nodded at the striking young woman sitting next to Kiersten. "Who is that?"

Cole was already shaking his head. "Don't even think about it."

Brooks leaned on the railing, his gaze intensifying. "Well, now you've piqued my interest."

Cole groaned. "I mean it, Brooks. That's Leah Andrews. She's one of Kiersten's oldest friends, and Piper's godmother. She's helping out with the baby this weekend until we find a permanent nanny. And you are not to touch."

"Hey. Poker club etiquette doesn't apply here. She's not an assistant, girlfriend, wife, or sister."

"Or mother."

"You really need to let that go."

Cole snorted. "She's Kiersten's friend. She will neuter you faster than you can squeal out your phone number."

"Oh, come on. Surely the lovely Leah can make her own decisions. She's not attached to anyone, is she?"

"I think she's going to be a nun."

Brooks raised an eyebrow. "A challenge. I like it. A nun? Really?"

Cole sighed and rubbed his forehead. "I don't know. Maybe she only works with nuns. At a school or something."

Brooks clutched his chest. "Oh my God, you're killing me. Seriously? A Catholic school teacher? Does she wear a uniform?"

Cole punched his arm and Brooks grunted. "Ow. Okay, okay. I'll lay off. Unless she comes on to me. I'm a gentleman, after all. Turning her down would be rude."

Cole laughed. "I should let you go for her just to watch Kiersten chew you up and spit you out. You know how she feels about you dating her friends."

Brooks sighed. "Yeah, yeah. Though I still maintain my innocence on that front."

"Right, because everything about you screams innocence."

Brooks flashed his best smile. "I don't know what you're talking about. I'm a total angel."

Kiersten looked up at the sound of her husband laughing and waved at him. Cole blew her a kiss.

Brooks groaned. "Oh, God. You've got it bad, don't you?"

"For my wife? Yes, yes I do."

Brooks shook his head again. In all honesty, he didn't blame Cole. Kiersten was a hell of a woman and there had been a brief, fleeting moment when Brooks could have imagined himself possibly trying for something other than his usual flings—before his friend had fallen head over heels in love with her, and she with him. Now, he was content to continue his eternally single ways. Most of the time.

He pushed away from the railing. "I can't watch that anymore. Come on," he said, towing his friend back toward the bar, "let's get another drink."

"Fine. But I mean it, Brooks. Leah is off-limits."

Because telling a man that a gorgeous woman was off-limits was the one surefire way to make sure he stayed away, right? No flaw in that logic at all.

• • •

Leah Andrews stared down at the sweet baby sleeping in her arms and tried not to vomit.

The rolling waves of morning sickness that hit her without warning were not meshing well with the literal rolling waves of the ocean. Though if she was going to be sick, she could definitely think of worse places to be. Floating around on a private yacht certainly beat lying around on her bathroom floor. Although, the bathroom, at least, was private.

The fresh air on the deck helped. She took a deep, shaky breath and tilted her face up to the sun. The sleepy little bundle of adorableness on her lap squirmed and she glanced down to make sure all was well.

"She doing okay?" Kiersten asked.

Leah smiled at her. "Your baby is perfect."

Kiersten smiled down at her offspring. "She is pretty perfect, isn't she?"

Leah laughed and handed the baby back to her mother. Kiersten Harrington was one of the few high school friends with whom Leah kept in contact, and she was seriously the luckiest woman alive. First, she'd done the impossible and won the lottery. Then she'd won the relationship lottery and married her gorgeous, billionaire boss. But, really, if it had to happen to anyone, Kiersten was a good one for it to happen to. She was a genuinely nice person, someone Leah had always felt she could turn to. And she'd never needed her more than she did now.

"How are you feeling?" Kiersten asked her.

Leah took stock of her stomach before answering. "Okay, I think. I was kind of iffy there for a second, but it's passed. I'd been feeling pretty great compared to the first couple months. Maybe the motion of the boat kick-started it again."

Kiersten gave her an indulgent smile. "I remember those days." She adjusted the baby in her arms. "You're past twelve weeks now, aren't you?"

Leah nodded, her hand cupping the tiny bump that was only just beginning to show. "Just barely."

"I'm glad you could help us this week. It's the first time I've been out of the house since Piper was born."

"Happy to. I could use the practice," she said with a wry smile.

"Have you heard from the father yet?"

Leah shook her head, keeping her gaze focused on the sea.

"Well…maybe he'll still contact you," Kiersten said, her voice bright with false hope.

"Maybe. Though as I told him, I'm fine if he doesn't. I think I'd prefer it. I don't know if he's read the letter yet. I had to message him on Facebook. It's a terrible way to tell someone they're going to be a father, but it's the only way I could get ahold of him. Didn't really expect my one-night stand to turn out like this. We never exchanged numbers. If he doesn't answer the message, I guess I can try asking people on his friends list. Though that would be awkward."

Kiersten patted her hand. "Just don't ever think you're alone, okay? You need help for anything, call me."

"I will," she said, giving Kiersten a grateful smile.

A shout of laughter came from further up the deck and the girls stopped chatting to see what was going on.

Brooks Larson, best friend and business partner of Kiersten's husband, sprinted up the deck with what looked like an octopus in his hands. A live, squirming octopus that he was using to chase two other men with. After he got a couple good squeals out of them, he dropped it back over the side.

Leah glanced at Kiersten who just grinned. "That's Brooks for you."

"Class clown?"

"Not really as bad as that, but he definitely likes to be amused."

Leah looked him over. The man was mouthwateringly gorgeous. Like some model or actor who was too insanely good-looking to be real. He'd give the Hemsworth brothers a run for their money. In fact, he was like the perfect mash-up. The coloring and chiseled features of Chris and the height and build of the slightly less buff Liam. With the good-natured goofiness of Dean from *Supernatural*. The man was perfection.

Or those could be the hormones talking. Either way, she'd never wanted to get up close and personal with a total stranger so badly in her life. She glanced back over at Kiersten, blushing when she realized her friend had been talking the whole time and she hadn't heard a word.

"Sorry. What was that?"

Kiersten grinned at her. "I said, you should go for it."

Leah frowned. "Go for what?"

Kiersten nodded over at where Brooks now leaned against the railing, drink in hand as he gazed out at the sparkling Mediterranean.

"What? You're crazy."

"Why? You're on vacation, have a little fun."

"I'm pregnant," Leah said, lowering her voice, though no one was close enough to hear them.

"I know," Kiersten said. "No reason to tell him that, though. You aren't looking for a baby daddy. Just a nice little send-off before the craziness begins."

Leah glanced back at Brooks. It was a crazy idea. But… maybe. She shook her head. "I can't. Besides, he might not even be interested."

"Oh, he's interested." Kiersten nodded over at him and Leah risked another look only to catch him staring at her with a soft smoldering smile that belonged on some Disney prince.

"Look," Kiersten said. "I'd normally be the last one to advocate something like this, but I know you. You've done nothing but obey the rules your whole life and the one time you step out of line…"

"I get pregnant," Leah finished for her. Yeah. She didn't miss the unfairness in it all. She'd always done everything right. Heck, even the little fling that had gotten her in her current predicament had been done by the book. She'd met a guy at a party hosted by good friends. He'd been a stranger, but he was a good, upstanding man as far as she could tell. A businessman based overseas in the city for a meeting. Didn't drink, at least in front of her. They'd gone into it both on the same page, and they'd used condoms. Several.

One hadn't worked.

"Right," Kiersten was saying. "But that's my point. When you get home, you'll be preparing for imminent parenthood and starting your new job at a private Catholic school of all places, so you'll never be able to have a lick of fun again. You might as well seize the opportunity while you can."

"Oh, ha ha," Leah said, though Kiersten wasn't all that wrong. Her employment came with a strict morality clause. Anxiety about what the school would do when they found out about her pregnancy kept her stomach in knots. They wouldn't be happy, but she hoped since she hadn't signed her employment agreement until after her one-night-stand-gone-wrong, there'd be some wiggle room. She'd come up with and rejected a dozen plans already. The thought of flat-out lying, saying she was a widow or had a husband who traveled, was a possibility, but not one that sat well with her. Her current plan involved doing the best damn job she could for the first few months, show them what an asset she could be. And then pray they'd be Christian enough to take pity on an unwed mother. There weren't many other jobs out there that offered free lodging and a good salary and healthcare. Losing it would hurt. She wouldn't be homeless. Kiersten wouldn't ever allow that to happen. But she didn't want to rely on her friend's charity. She was going to make her own way in the world. Build a life for her and the baby.

Before she could respond further to Kiersten's suggestion, a shadow fell over her. She glanced up right into the sky-blue eyes of the man in question.

# Chapter Two

Brooks smiled down at Leah, loving the slight blush that stained her cheeks. She had that innocent, good-girl vibe emanating off her like a homing beacon. He didn't know why that was such a turn-on. Maybe because it was different. He typically steered clear of the good girls; too many complications. And he had a strict policy of only getting involved with women who were as commitment-phobic as he was. It made life easier.

But he'd been watching Leah all morning and couldn't get her out of his head. The yacht was crawling with people. A pre-christening party for his goddaughter. When Cole had mentioned they were bringing someone to help with the baby, Brooks had pictured some heavyset matriarch wielding diapers and wet wipes. Not this brown-eyed beauty that blinked up at him with a shy smile. How could he possibly resist that?

Besides, Kiersten was smiling, not glaring any warnings at him. That was a green light in his book.

"I don't think we've met yet," he said, extending a hand.

"I'm Brooks Larson. Their second in command," he said, nodding at Kiersten and Cole, who had come up behind her.

"Leah Andrews," she said. "Their nanny for the weekend."

He took her hand, holding it rather than shaking it. "It's a very great pleasure to meet you," he said, laying on the charm as thick as he dared.

"Likewise," she said, her fingers tightening around his ever so slightly.

Hmm, intriguing. He'd expected her to be a bit shy. And while her voice was quiet, it was strong, straightforward. Confident and sexy as hell.

"Would you care for a walk around the deck before the party really gets underway? I saw the DJ setting up near the bow, but there's a perfect spot to view the islands from the stern."

"That sounds great," she said, glancing back at Cole and Kiersten. "If you don't need me right now?"

Cole glanced at his wife, his forehead slightly creased, but Kiersten grinned. "Go on. It's about time for me to feed Piper anyway."

Brooks held out his hand and waited for Leah to take it. He wasn't completely sure she would, which was an unusual experience for him. He was young, rich, and good-looking—that was a winning trifecta right there.

The woman before him, however, was not his usual prey. For one thing, she took care of children for a living, which typically meant she was a responsible adult. Responsible adults rarely had fun. And Brooks liked to have fun. She also had a bright-eyed innocent look about her. Unlike some of the other guests who were lounging in bikinis and sarongs while sipping champagne, Leah wore a cute sundress, complete with a gold crucifix necklace, and was drinking what looked like an ice water with lemon. Not the type he usually went for and certainly not the type that went for him.

"You look confused," she said, slipping her hand into his.

"Maybe a little," he said with a short laugh. "Kiersten just smiling and encouraging you to go off with me instead of beating me off with a stick is unusual."

"Hmm, should I be worried?" she asked, though her tone remained flirtatious.

"Not at all. I'm a pretty decent guy. Just not looking for anything serious."

"Why do I feel like you're trying to make a good impression in a job interview?"

Brooks gave her his best aw-shucks-you-caught-me grin. "Well, it's not a job interview, but I am trying to make a good impression."

"Really?"

"Really. How am I doing?"

Leah took a sip of her water and shrugged. "The jury's still out. I'll let you know."

That surprised a laugh out of him. "I guess I'll have to try harder."

"Or you could be yourself and we'll go from there."

Brooks lifted his glass in a small salute. "A novel approach."

"Sometimes the simplest line of attack is the most efficient."

"Wouldn't it have been even more efficient to gather intel on me from Kiersten?"

"You're assuming I didn't already do that."

Another surprise. She was full of them. "And she didn't tell you to run screaming in the other direction as fast as possible."

Leah laughed, a throaty, rippling sound that was both infectious and sexy. "No, she didn't. But even if she had, I can make my own decisions."

He leaned in a little closer. "Then I guess I should be thankful both for your impeccable decision-making capabilities and for Kiersten not throwing me under the bus."

Leah shrugged. "Maybe she thought we should get to know each other since I'm Piper's godmother. The godparents should know each other, I suppose."

"True."

"Or, maybe she thought I was a big girl and could handle you," Leah said. At his raised brow, she grinned. "Or at least handle myself."

"Is that right?"

Leah stopped and leaned an elbow against the railing. He followed suit, standing much closer than necessary. She didn't move away.

"I get it. I know what I look like. Sweet little inexperienced Catholic girl. Naive, innocent." His gaze raked over her and she shrugged. "See, men assume because I'm quiet, dress a little conservatively, and go to church most Sundays that I'm an innocent child who needs to be guided and protected. It's infuriating, and a little creepy."

"For the record, the thought never crossed my mind that you were a child."

She gave him an eye-rolling grin.

"So, what are you then, assuming most men's assumptions are wrong?"

Her expression was a curious mixture of shy confidence. "A full-grown woman who can take care of herself."

Brooks grinned. "Point taken. So, oh experienced woman of the world, what do you do for a living? Cole mentioned something about becoming a nun?"

Leah opened her mouth, then grinned, a slight blush staining her cheeks. "No, I am not becoming a nun. I'm a teacher at a private girls' school run by nuns."

Brooks burst out laughing. "You're not even making that

up, are you?"

Leah laughed. "Okay, fine. I guess I fit the stereotype a little. Hush."

"What's a nice girl like you doing hanging out with a boatful of heathens like us?" he asked, nodding at the people milling about on the boat.

"The 'heathens' you're referring to aren't exactly the scum of the earth," she said with a laugh. "Aside from their obscene bank accounts, they all seem pretty nice. Most of them, anyway," she said, looking him up and down.

He gave her a slow smile with as much smolder as he could lay on and returned her roving gaze. Instead of blushing and backing off, she moved a little closer.

"Besides," she said, "even nice girls like to have some fun. I'm on a yacht in the middle of the Mediterranean with good friends, celebrating the birth of my goddaughter. Can't think of any place I'd rather be. It was good of you to host this getaway for them."

A rush of pride flooded through him, something he didn't feel very often. He liked that she approved of him. It had been a long time since he'd cared about what anyone thought. He didn't know what it was about her, but she intrigued him, which scared the hell out of him, truthfully. But that paled in comparison to his desire to get to know her better. Much better.

"She's my goddaughter and they're my best friends. It was the least I could do. Besides, I'm always up for a party."

She smiled at that, though the expression didn't quite reach her eyes, and then looked out at the view spread before them. They weren't far from land, so the whitewashed walls and blue roofs of the Greek village they were passing twinkled at them from the shores of the bay. The crystal-clear turquoise waters beneath them beckoned invitingly though a sudden cool breeze blew through, sending a fine shiver through Leah.

Brooks moved behind her, sheltering her with his body, his hands resting beside hers on the railing. "What are you thinking about so hard?" he asked, bending down so he could talk quietly. The scent of her hair washed over him. Honeysuckle and jasmine. He inhaled deeply, imprinting the scent in his mind.

"The future," she said. Instead of moving away as he'd feared, she leaned back into him. A slight movement, but encouraging, though the future was a subject he tended to avoid as much as possible.

"Why think of the future when the present is so much more stimulating?" He ran a hand up her arm and she turned until she faced him.

"You don't find the future stimulating?"

"When I have a beautiful woman in my arms right now?" He drew his thumb over her cheek. "Why would I want to think of anything else?"

His heart pounded while he waited for her to push him away, giggle and blush maybe, play hard to get. Or get offended and stomp off in a huff. He didn't expect her to tilt her face against his hand so he cradled her cheek. The sun highlighted her hair, illuminating shades of red and blonde that reminded him of the fine mahogany table he had in his office. He brushed a strand away from her eyes, pools of brown with subtle flecks of green that had him mesmerized.

What had she done to him? He'd never wanted to kiss a woman so badly in his life. He leaned down, his pulse speeding. She gave him a gentle, encouraging smile, then froze. Her eyes widened, all the color in her face draining, and before he could ask what was wrong she pivoted and leaned far over the rail, her body tensing as she threw up what looked like everything she'd ever eaten.

He grabbed her hair, gathering it at the nape of her neck

and holding it with one hand while he held her against him with his other arm, supporting her while she retched. Kiersten was at their side almost immediately with a towel and a bottle of water. He took both from her, ignoring her shocked face.

Leah took the towel gratefully and quickly rinsed out her mouth. Brooks led her over to a chair and ordered one of the passing waiters to bring him a glass of ice water with mint leaves. Kiersten's eyes widened in question.

"I read somewhere that mint calms the stomach. And the flavor might help get the taste out of her mouth," he said.

Kiersten looked like she was going to respond, but ended up shaking her head with a small smile. Brooks knew exactly what she was thinking, but ignored everyone other than Leah. Kiersten watched them for a moment and then went back to where Cole held the baby, a speculative gleam in her eye that he'd defuse later.

The waiter returned quickly, and Leah slowly sipped the mint water a few times before sighing deeply.

"Thank you," she said, not meeting his eyes.

"Was the thought of kissing me that horrible?" he asked, smiling, though part of him really wondered if that had been the case.

Her gaze shot to his. "No, not at all!"

"Motion sickness?" They were on a boat after all.

She sighed again. "More like morning sickness." She put the glass down, sat up straight, and looked him dead in the eye. "I'm pregnant."

# Chapter Three

Leah watched his expression go from blank to surprised with what she swore was a moment of panic.

Brooks stared at her for a moment before the usual goofball glimmer was back in his eyes. "Don't we have to sleep together first? Or am I drunker than I thought?"

Her lips twitched, but she was not going to reward that remark with a laugh. And now that the cat was out of the bag it was probably time to move on and get ready for the christening anyway.

She stood and nodded to him where he still knelt at the side of the chair. "It was nice to meet you."

"Wait," he said, standing and catching her hand before she could make it too far away. "Sorry. Bad joke."

She shook her head. "It's okay. Just…a little awkward to nearly throw up on a guy you were seconds from kissing."

Her cheeks heated up, but she tried to ignore it. She blushed at the drop of a hat. Always had. To say it was irritating would be an understatement.

He still held her hand. She glanced down at where he was

entwining his fingers with hers and then back up to meet his gaze, her eyes wide in question.

"We were seconds from kissing, weren't we?" he asked, drawing her closer. "I'm definitely going to need a rain check when you're feeling better."

"Oh, I'm fine now. Once I…you know, I actually feel pretty good for a while."

"Well then," he said, pulling her against him with a grin. "If you're feeling better…"

He bent down and she pulled from his grasp, hand clapped over her mouth. She'd just puked over the side of the boat. She was *not* going to start making out with him *now*. "That's not what I meant," she said with a little laugh.

"Why?"

"Because."

"That's not an answer."

"Sure it is. Just not one you like."

He grinned. "This is true. So give me another one."

She pressed her lips together to keep her smile in check and put her hand on his chest to push him away. "Now isn't a good time."

"Now is always a good time." He paused, frowning slightly. "Would the father object? I mean, is he—"

"He's not in the picture." No matter what he decided he wanted his role to be with the baby, if she could ever get ahold of him, they weren't in a relationship and she had no plans for them to ever be.

"Well, then…"

"We've got to get ready for the christening." And she had to brush her teeth before she got anywhere near him again.

Brooks checked his watch, then frowned and sighed. "I guess we do. Well then, I'll meet you in front of your cabin in half an hour so I can escort you to the boats that will take us ashore."

"That's not necessary."

"It would be my pleasure." He brought her hand to his lips and kissed it like some medieval knight.

Okay, he was kind of over the top but still…*swoon*.

"Besides," he said. "We're the godparents. We'll have to stand together at the church. Might as well arrive together."

She couldn't argue with that, though she had no idea why he'd still want to spend time in her company now that he knew she was pregnant.

"All right, then. Half an hour."

He gave her a playful wink that had her stomach flip-flopping. Or maybe it was just another round of morning sickness. Either way, it would probably be best to quickly make her escape.

Not that escape seemed possible.

When she opened her cabin door to head to the boats that would take them ashore, Brooks was there waiting. He sat beside her on the boat and helped her to the shore, and then insisted on escorting her into the small stone chapel on the banks of the tiny Greek island owned by one of Cole's friends.

The amount of money in the collective bank accounts of the people in that church blew her mind. Part of her envied what Kiersten and Cole would be able to give their child. They'd never have to worry about finding a decent—and affordable—place to live, or good childcare, or any of the necessities of life. Not to mention all the fun stuff like the latest toys and trendy clothes. That kind of security would be amazing.

But there were some downsides to growing up filthy rich. All she had to do was look around the gathering. Granted, the people streaming into the church were better than many of their subset. Cole and Kiersten were good people and they wouldn't have invited anyone who wasn't more like them than not. Still, there was more than a fair share of trophy wives dripping in diamonds carrying Tiffany gift bags for the new baby. Because that's what every baby needed—a literal silver spoon or two to play with. Even the nicer ones in the bunch seemed a bit out of touch with real, everyday life.

Leah felt like a regular Joe in a sea of Gwyneth Paltrows. They might be nice and mean well, but they still thought a hundred dollars for a T-shirt was a steal and didn't blink an eye at spending a cool grand on a onesie their kid would puke on inside of five minutes. Leah might have to struggle sometimes, but at least her child wouldn't grow up spoiled and out of touch with reality.

Though…a little of that unrealistic fantasy might be nice. Struggling on her own was bad enough. The thought of being responsible for another human being filled her with terror.

All further musings on the impending doom in her life ceased the moment Kiersten handed her baby Piper. Leah smiled down at her goddaughter. People say all babies are cute. People also know that isn't remotely true. There are some unfortunate newborns out there. Piper, however, resided firmly in the adorable zone. Especially at that moment, with her flowing christening gown and matching bonnet, her rosy round cheeks sweetly dimpled, cupid's-bow lips puckered with sleepy phantom sucking.

Leah took a deep breath. Yes. There were many aspects of her impending motherhood that made her want to go into the fetal position herself. But then again, in six months' time, she'd be holding her own tiny bundle of adorableness. It had its perks.

She looked up at the proud parents, not even caring about the dopey grin on her face. Until her gaze met that of Brooks who, as godfather, stood right beside her.

He watched her, his brow drawn slightly. Like she was a puzzle he couldn't figure out. She mentally snorted. *Get in line, buddy.*

• • •

The after-christening soiree was in full swing under the tent that had been set up on the beach, the twinkling white lights that had been strung all over anything that didn't move creating an intensely romantic atmosphere. Prime seduction real estate, right there. But the only woman he was even remotely interested in seducing was cradling the guest of honor who had apparently decided it was past her bedtime and had fallen asleep in Leah's arms. Not that he blamed the little thing. Falling asleep in Leah's arms, after doing a few other things there, was currently top on his bucket list.

Of course, he still couldn't quite wrap his head around the thought that she had one of those little creatures growing in her belly. Why he hadn't shaken her hand and immediately hauled ass away from her the moment she'd told him she was pregnant was a mystery he didn't want to delve into just then. His interest still burned strong, bad idea or not. Maybe *because* it was a bad idea. He was obtuse like that. Whatever the reason, he couldn't get Leah out of his head.

She finally handed the baby back to Kiersten, a curious expression on her face. Like she both longed for and dreaded the idea of someone handing her own baby back to her, which, thankfully, wasn't something that would be happening anytime soon. They still had time to have a little fun first. And now that her attention wasn't occupied…

He downed the rest of his champagne, keeping his gaze zeroed in on her until she looked up. He put on his best swagger and headed straight for her. She watched him approach like he was a lion stalking his prey. Or…maybe a giraffe would be more like it. Did giraffes have prey? Either way, with his height, he'd always been more Deadpool than Wolverine in the body department. And if she got that reference, he'd marry her on the spot.

"Dance with me," he said, holding a hand out to her.

Her eyes widened at the command. "Didn't your mother ever teach you how to ask nicely?"

He gave her a slow grin. "Of course, but I figured if I asked that would give you room to turn me down, and I don't want that."

"You always get what you want?"

"Generally, yes."

"Sounds like you could use a lesson in patience."

He pulled her up and into his arms. "Always the teacher, hmm?"

She grimaced a bit. "I try not to be. Can't seem to help myself."

He swayed with her to the music. "Don't stop on my account. I'm finding the whole schoolteacher thing erotic."

She snorted. "I think you find pretty much everything erotic."

"If it's to do with you, absolutely." He twirled her and she gripped his shoulders. It was all he could do not to haul her against him and show her exactly how erotic he found her. She laughed, despite the obvious effort she was making to keep it together. That quiet, husky sound made him want to really amp her up so he could hear it again. At a louder volume.

He spun her away from him and brought her back, continuing their path along the dance floor.

She glanced around them and then back up at him. "Every woman in here is staring at you. You could have any one of them. Why are you dancing with me?"

He met her gaze. "Because I like you."

Her eyes narrowed slightly. "You don't even know me."

"I like what I know so far and am trying to get to know you better. If you could stop making that so difficult it would be much appreciated."

Her lips twitched. "You already know the most important thing about me."

He lifted his brows. "I do?"

She let out an exasperated sigh. "I'm pregnant."

"I know."

"And you're still here dancing with me."

He frowned again. "Is there any reason I shouldn't?"

That seemed to confuse her. "I don't know. I figured the whole baby thing would scare the hell out of most guys."

"Why? Is it contagious? Is it going to rub off on me or something?"

The lips twitched into a half grin. "No."

"Are you in imminent danger of giving birth right here on the dance floor?"

"Of course not."

He pulled her closer. "Then I see no reason why we can't have a little fun."

The shy but happy smile she gave him nearly stopped him in his tracks. That smile was like a firefly blinking in a pitch-dark room. Quiet, subtle, and breathtakingly beautiful. The lone spot of light in his world. There was little he wouldn't do to keep that smile on her face.

"Tell me something you want," he said, leaning down to whisper in her ear.

She pulled back enough to meet his gaze. "What?"

"Anything. You name it. The night is ours."

She shrugged, that small smile still in place. "What more could I want? I'm surrounded by friends, on a gorgeous island in the middle of the Mediterranean, in a tent stuffed with the best food I've ever tasted in my life. Seriously, Kiersten needs to give that caterer a massive tip."

She stopped dancing and met his gaze. "And the most handsome man in the room has been trying to make me smile all night. There are worse ways to spend the evening."

He drew a finger along her cheek until he cupped her jaw and drew her forward slowly enough that she could pull away if she wanted to. His heart did a serious fist bump when she leaned into him instead.

"Let's see if we can make the evening even better." Before he could taste the sweet lips that were mere inches from his own, someone clapped him on the shoulder. "Hey, mate," a slightly slurred British voice said.

Brooks closed his eyes and took a deep breath. "Harrison, what can I do for you?"

Harrison Troy had been a good friend and member of his poker club for years now. Aside from Cole, Harrison was probably his best friend. But, hey, everyone had to die sometime. They'd had a good run. If he didn't walk away right that instant so Brooks could get back to what he'd been about to do, things were going to get ugly.

"Who is this lovely young lady?" Harrison asked, looking Leah up and down.

"This is Leah," Brooks said, keeping her in his arms, but putting her slightly behind him. Not that she needed protection from Harrison; he was true-born British gentry. Unless she had an urgent need to duel to the death with a fencing saber, she was probably safe from old Harry. Harrison, however, was not going to be safe from Brooks if he didn't make himself scarce.

"Leah." Harrison took her hand and kissed it. "Pleasure to meet you."

"The pleasure's all mine," she said.

"It was about to be," Brooks muttered.

Leah's jaw dropped and Brooks winked at her. Then he went back to glaring at Harrison.

"Kiersten was looking for you," Harrison said to Leah. "I believe she needs help with the guest of honor."

"Of course," Leah said, pulling away from Brooks. Only he wasn't ready to let her go yet. He kept a grip on her hand.

"Excuse us," he said to Harrison. He pulled Leah out of the tent, ignoring her little squeak of surprise. He led her far enough away that they were out of the circle of light, down near the shoreline where the waves lapped gently at the beach.

"Brooks, what—"

He cut off her words with his lips and thank Dionysus or Pan or whatever drunk, frolicking god the ancient Greeks had worshipped, she kissed him back. Good God, did she kiss him back. That delectable little mouth of hers opened beneath his and ravished him, inside and out. He couldn't suck enough air into his lungs, but there was no way in hell he was pulling away from her to breathe. Keeping his lips fused to hers was far more important than some measly need for oxygen.

She broke away first, her chest heaving, eyes wide. Before he could say a word, she wrapped her hands in his lapels and hauled him back to her, kissing him hard and fast. Then she gave him a playful push, grinned like a mischievous child, and ran back into the tent.

Brooks stood staring after her for so long he lost track of time, though it probably wasn't more than a few moments. The tent beckoned, warm light, good food, and the laughter of his friends spilling out into the night. He needed to get his head on straight, though, before he went near the public.

Before he managed to do that, Cole came and found him, staring at him with a furrowed forehead for a minute before finally asking, "What's up?"

Brooks still hadn't taken his eyes off the spot where Leah

had disappeared. "Shhh," he said. "I'm having a Disney princess moment."

Cole's eyebrows hit his hairline. "Do I want to know what that means?"

"Probably not."

"You going to tell me anyway?"

Brooks opened his mouth, closed it, opened it again, searching for the words to describe what had just happened. And failing. He sighed. "No one has ever kissed me like that before. No one. *Ever.*"

Cole nodded his head, not speaking for a minute. For a brief, glorious moment, Brooks thought he might not get any shit from his friend. As usual, he was wrong.

"So, you talking the whole floating hearts and fireworks going off over your head or the leg-pop thing?" Cole turned sideways and lifted his leg in the perfect imitation of a thoroughly kissed damsel.

"Fuck off," Brooks said with a laugh.

Cole chuckled. "You started it with that Disney princess bullshit."

Brooks sighed. "Yeah. There might have been fireworks, though, but don't tell anyone. My rep would be totally ruined."

"Your secret is safe with me."

Cole watched him a minute longer, then asked, "Fireworks, huh?"

"Yup."

"What are you going to do about it?"

Brooks sighed. "Get blind fucking drunk until the urge to run after her and beg her to spend the rest of her life kissing me has passed."

Cole shrugged. "It might not be all that bad, you know."

For the first time in his life, Brooks agreed. And that thought sent a bolt of terror through him so strong it was all he could do not to jump in the water, swim back to his yacht, and head for the nearest uninhabited island. Brooks wasn't relationship material and he damn well knew it. Hell, he prided himself on it. Leah wasn't just regular relationship material either; she was going to be a mom. Even if he could change enough to be a decent boyfriend, no kid deserved to have him hanging around messing things up.

"She's better off without me," Brooks said, shoving the disappointed twinge those words caused back into the deep, dark box where it belonged.

Cole handed him the champagne flute in his hand. "Then I suppose we should go get you drunk."

Brooks downed the champagne in one gulp and followed Cole back into the tent. Although it was totally useless. There wasn't enough booze in the world to make him forget that kiss. Or the woman who'd given it to him.

# Chapter Four

Leah pulled up to the curb in front of the school where she would be teaching. If you could call it a school. The place looked more like a castle someone had dropped on the outskirts of the city, complete with a ten-foot stone wall enclosing the campus.

It had always been her dream to teach at a school like this. All she could do was hope the consequences of the one night she'd decided to be totally crazy wouldn't derail all her plans. She needed the job now more than ever.

"No worries, little peanut," she muttered in the vague direction of her belly. "I'll take care of everything. Everything's going to work out fine."

She would make sure of it.

She sighed and shut off her car, taking a minute to check her phone to see if any messages had come through yet. Nothing from Marcus Cassidy, the man who still didn't know he was going to be a father. She didn't know what else to try. The only reason she knew his full name was because she'd seen his driver's license the night she'd been with him.

They hadn't exchanged any info. That had been part of the whole tantalizing night, not knowing each other, keeping it a mystery. At the time, it had been exciting. Now…yeah, not so much.

Finding him on Facebook had been a miracle, but he had everything on his profile set to private. She couldn't see his friends list, any of his posts, nothing. All she could do was keep sending message requests and hope he answered one.

There were no messages from the other man either. Brooks. The goofball prince with more money than God, and more charm than anyone had the right to have, who had kissed her senseless and then disappeared from her life, which was for the best, she knew. The last thing she needed was another complication—and Brooks had complication written all over him.

Still, it was an ego blow to have him pursue her all over the Mediterranean only to drop her like a toad that had peed on his hand the second she gave in. She'd known kissing him was a mistake; she hadn't been able to help herself. And for her, it had been amazing. Beyond amazing. It had been weeks and she still thought about it every damn day and dreamed about it most nights, too. Apparently, he hadn't felt the same way. Maybe she'd had bad breath. Or that last kiss before she'd run off had been too forward. Or running off had given him the wrong impression, even though he'd known she had to go.

"Or maybe I'm way overthinking something that doesn't matter," she said, climbing out of the car before she could get derailed on any more trains of thought.

The campus was quiet this time of day, especially since school hadn't yet begun for the year. She wasn't too concerned about parking against the curb. It wouldn't take her too long to unload and there weren't many people around anyway. A parking lot sat a few feet away, but she had some boxes to haul and every foot closer she could get to her quarters, the better.

Three trips later and she wished she'd driven her damn car right up to her door. She dropped the boxes in her arms onto the counter of her small kitchen and took a second to breathe. Just a few more left. Though, unfortunately, they were the heavy ones. Mostly books, far too many books. She was cheerfully addicted to reading, but even she had to admit it made moving difficult, at least without a few strong men to haul the boxes around.

She took a deep breath and headed back out. The sooner she finished, the sooner she could plop down on the couch with a pint of mint chocolate chip ice cream and veg out to a chick flick or two.

Leah went back through the old corridor that led to the parking lot. She loved the architecture of this place. It made her feel like she lived in an old monastery or something. Though the building was nowhere near as old as those in Europe, the stone walls and landscaped courtyards still embodied the atmosphere of ancient beauty. What an incredible place to raise her baby.

If they let her keep her job.

The familiar thrum of panic rolled through her system. She couldn't lose this job. She had nowhere to go, no money saved up aside from what Kiersten had insisted on paying her for her help that weekend. Which had been unnecessary and far too generous, but she had to admit, it eased a little of her stress to have something in the bank. She'd have to hope that the headmistress took pity on her. She was a good teacher. Maybe she could make herself so indispensable, her pregnancy wouldn't matter.

She walked through the arched gate in the wall and stopped short. Brooks had pulled up behind her car and stood leaning against it, waiting for her.

"Hey!" he called, one of those heart-tripping smiles he excelled at spreading across his lips.

What the hell was he doing there? He'd kissed her silly and then totally disappeared from her life, and now he'd decided to show up, at her home and place of business, and she was supposed to what, swoon? Throw herself in his arms? Giggle and faint because he decided she was worthy of his attention after all?

Apparently, she'd been a little angrier over his silence than she'd realized, which made the whole thing a really bad idea. Scratch that. Having him there was like a bad idea on steroids. Her hands practically itched to trace the hard planes of his body. It had been weeks and she still couldn't resist his pull. The man was like smooth whiskey, dipped in chocolate, sprinkled with coffee, and rolled in a fountain of sugar. All the unbelievably delicious things she craved and couldn't have.

She ignored him and opened the rear door to gather the bags on the backseat. Maybe if she didn't acknowledge his presence, he'd go away. She didn't have time for the emotional and physical rodeo she'd been going through since the christening trip, not to mention the bucking bronco in her gut every time she was within fifty feet of the man.

She should have known ignoring him wouldn't work. Brooks didn't seem the type to take rejection. He was far too aware of his appeal for his own good.

Leah slung her garment bag over one shoulder, then grabbed the nearest box from the trunk and hefted it up.

"Let me carry that," Brooks said, hot on her heels.

She glanced down at his empty arms. "This would go a lot faster if you'd carry the other boxes instead of worrying about me carrying this one. I'm fine."

"It's heavy. You should let me carry it for you. In fact, you should have just hired someone to move all this stuff for you."

Leah snorted. "Right. I'm going to spend a few hundred dollars I don't have for a few boxes? It's not that far. I'm fine."

He made a swipe for the box and she yanked it away. Before he could try again, she turned left through the arched entryway to the corridor that contained her quarters and came to a stop in front of the first door.

"See. We're already there. Open the door, will you?"

He frowned, but opened the door, pushing it wide so she could go in. She marched the box straight to the coffee table in her small living room and dropped it. She didn't want Brooks to see, but carrying that box had winded her a little. Or maybe it had been their game of keep away. No matter. She was perfectly capable of carrying the rest. She wasn't stupid enough to risk injuring herself or the baby to prove a point, but the boxes really weren't that heavy.

"You're stubborn, you know that?"

"And you're a borderline stalker," she said.

"Am not."

She bit her lip, resisting the urge to join in with the "Am not, am too" game.

"What are you doing here, Brooks?"

He shrugged. "I wanted to talk to you."

"Why now? I haven't heard from you since the trip, and now you want to talk to me so badly you show up here instead of calling?"

"I would have, but I wasn't all that sure you'd answer."

"I wouldn't have."

She so would have, but he sure as hell didn't need to know that. The amused grin he aimed at her made it clear he already knew it.

She glared at him and spun on her heel back out the door.

"I'll get the rest," Brooks said, heading her off.

She stopped and planted her hands on her hips. "I can get them myself. Seriously, why are you here? You didn't come to say hi or carry my boxes for me. How did you know I'd be here today anyway?"

"Kiersten told Cole. Cole told me."

Leah frowned. "Traitors."

Brooks stepped closer and she stood her ground, though the effort it took sent a fine tremor through her legs.

"Are you really so pissed that I'm here?"

"Yes," she said, though the word barely made it out of her throat.

Brooks gave her that slow, sexy grin that made her knees melt into a pile of goo.

"I don't believe you." He leaned down and brushed his lips just at the corner of her lips.

Her mouth dropped open in a little sigh and he cupped her face in his hands, going in for something deeper.

"No." She pushed him away and held up a hand to keep him back. If he kissed her, she was a goner. She was trying to keep her job at the school, not get kicked out for making out in the corridors.

He held his hands up in surrender though his gaze burned into hers. He knew exactly the effect he had on her.

"I have to get the rest of the things."

"I told you, I'll get them," he said, easily overtaking her.

She followed him, jogging a little to keep up with his long stride. She made it to the car half a second behind him.

He gave her an exasperated grimace.

"Oh, relax," she said, reaching into the car for another box. "There's only two left and this way we'll be done in one trip."

"I could carry them both and we'd still be done in one trip."

She hefted it to her hip and took off. "Too late," she called over her shoulder.

She laughed at his muffled curse and sped up.

"Leah," he said, catching up with almost no effort at all. Maybe she was a little more winded than she realized. "This is ridiculous."

"Yes, it is." She turned into her corridor. "We are already at the apartment so there's no point in you harping on this. What is the big deal with me carrying a couple boxes? I'm not dying I'm just preg…"

She turned into her apartment and froze at the sight of the headmistress, Mother Genevieve, standing there. "…nant," she finished, the rest of the word nearly choking her.

"Right, and pregnant women shouldn't be—" Brooks entered the room and stopped short at the woman standing there. "Carrying boxes."

He put down his box and then took Leah's from her. She didn't take her eyes from the nun in front of her. Well…she'd needed to tell her eventually. Sooner was probably better than later.

"Mother Genevieve…" Leah started.

"Is this true?" the headmistress asked. "Are you pregnant?"

Leah took a deep breath, trying to calm the roiling of her stomach. "Yes, but…"

"You've broken the moral code of your contract before it's even begun? That is a record, I must say."

"No, I didn't. Really."

"Then you lied in your interview when you assured us there were no impediments to your being hired."

"No. I never lied."

Mother Genevieve frowned. "I don't see how you can possibly have it both ways. Which is it?"

Leah straightened her back, refusing to flinch away from the judgment in the woman's eyes. "I became pregnant before you hired me and I signed the morality agreement, but I had not yet discovered my condition when you interviewed me. I would not knowingly lie about such a thing, Mother Genevieve. Even if I wanted to, it would be pointless. It isn't something I can exactly hide."

Brooks moved closer to her. Not touching her, but enough that she could feel his presence at her back. Interestingly enough, it buoyed her courage in the face of the holy condemnation currently raining down on her.

"Yes, you are right on that point. And that is precisely where our problem lies. I'm afraid I have to ask you to leave the premises immediately. We rescind our offer of employment."

Leah's stomach dropped, all her worst fears barreling toward her at once. "Mother Genevieve, please—"

"I'm sorry, Miss Andrews, but you knew the conditions of this position when it was offered to you."

"I know. I did. And like I said, I wouldn't knowingly deceive you…"

"You couldn't possibly believe that we'd allow this to go unchallenged."

"Well, no, but I'd hoped… I need this job, Mother."

The old nun sighed. "I'm sorry, my hands are tied. We cannot have an unwed mother teach here. What kind of example would that set for our students?"

"But Mother—"

"She's not unwed. She's married," Brooks said, wrapping his arm around her waist. "To me."

# Chapter Five

The looks of shock on both Leah's and the nun's faces were nothing compared to what was going on inside Brooks's own head. What the hell had possessed him to say that?

The only defense he had was that he couldn't stand Leah's distress or the judgmental disdain with which the old headmistress had looked at her. So he'd said the first thing that came to his head, the only thing that would fix the problem. Leah needed a husband. Now she had one. Sort of.

"You are her husband?" Mother Genevieve asked, looking him up and down. "Then why didn't she mention you before? And why did she require single unit housing? I'm afraid a divorced pregnant teacher isn't much better..."

"We aren't divorced," Leah started, obviously heading straight for the truth.

"I'm afraid I don't understand," the headmistress said, her aggravation mounting.

"We aren't married yet," Brooks said. "We will be shortly. Does that change things?" He drew Leah closer to him, squeezing her waist and willing her to be quiet.

Mother Genevieve looked at them, her thin lips pursed. "I suppose so. It's quite unorthodox. You will need to be married with your marriage certificate on file before the school year begins. And we'll need to review your living arrangements."

"I can make other arrangements for her," Brooks said, earning another glare from Leah.

Mother Genevieve nodded. "Indeed. I'm not sure why a woman on the verge of marriage and motherhood requested living quarters for just herself but…"

"I travel a lot for work so we thought it best that she stays here on campus." He flinched at a sharp pinch from Leah. "We will change our plans. I can find her…us…something close to campus."

The headmistress nodded again. "Very well." She sighed and rubbed her temples. "I do hope the rest of your tenure with us is a little less…confusing, Miss Andrews. Or would that be Mrs.?"

"Mrs. Larson," Brooks said, his lips going numb with the magnitude of what he'd done being spelled out in such a way. "Soon to be." He forced a smile.

Mother Genevieve gave them a sharp nod and swept out. The moment they were alone, Leah pulled away and rounded on him.

"What the hell are you doing?"

"Whoa, Mrs. Larson. I don't think you're allowed to use that kind of language here."

Holy shit, did he just call her Mrs. Larson? What the hell *was* he doing?

"You're insane, you know that?" Leah started pacing, her arms wrapped around herself like she was physically trying to hold herself together.

She had a point. This was totally insane. He opened his mouth to agree, but what came out was, "What? You needed a husband. Now you have one."

*Where did that come from?* It was like his mouth was on autopilot.

She stared at him. "You can't possibly mean to go through with this."

Of course he didn't. "Hell yeah, I do."

He couldn't make it stop.

"And what do you mean, you'll find us a place? You're going to buy a new home because I need a place close to campus?"

This one was easy, at least.

"No need. My loft isn't that far from here. Not as close as living on campus, of course. But a fifteen-minute commute, tops, and my drivers will always be at your disposal."

"Why didn't you tell the Mother Superior that?"

"Because she'd have asked why you weren't staying there in the first place."

"As opposed to the *massive* white lie you'd already told? Or would that be a massive scarlet letter lie? I'm so going to hell."

Brooks raised an eyebrow. "Well, that's a little melodramatic."

She glared at him. "It is not. We are deceiving my boss *who is a nun*. I think you get extra hell points for that."

"I don't think God is sitting around all day keeping score."

She ignored that remark. "You can't move me into your house and have your drivers at my beck and call every day."

"Why not?"

Leah stopped in front of him. "Brooks, this isn't some joke. It's not something we can fake our way through. She wants a marriage certificate on file. A real marriage certificate. There's only one way to get one of those."

His stomach did a great impression of a skydiver without

a parachute. He was *not* marriage material. He'd spent most his adult life proving that fact over and over. He had no business whatsoever even saying his name and marriage in the same sentence. And yet…he looked down into the wide, fear-filled eyes of the woman in front of him. She needed his help. And for once in his life, he was going to step up and do something about it.

"Then let's go get us a marriage certificate."

"We barely know each other."

He waggled his eyebrows at her. "Well, if we're getting married, we can get to know each other a lot better."

She threw up her hands. "I am not marrying you, you crazy person!"

"Why not? Marriage could be fun."

"Marriage isn't supposed to be fun. Marriage is serious."

"It doesn't have to be."

She sighed and shook her head. "Brooks…"

"Come here," he said, taking her hand and drawing her over to the couch. "Look, I know the marriage certificate has to be real, but that doesn't mean the marriage has to be."

She frowned. "What do you mean?"

"I mean, we get married, show the old bat her marriage certificate, and then at some point we can get the marriage annulled. No one has to know about that part. We said I travel a lot so it's not like they'll be expecting me to show up regularly."

Leah put her face in her hands. "This is crazy."

Yes. Yes it was. No need to harp on that though or he'd talk them out of it. Instead, he got down on his knees and pulled her hands from her face. "Come on, Leah. Be my fake wife. What have you got to lose?"

She laughed a little. "My sanity? My dignity?"

He waved those off. "Overrated."

Her smile faded a little around the edges. "Why are you

doing this for me? What do you get out of it?"

*You.*

He squashed that thought immediately. She was great and all, but he didn't need or want her. Not permanently anyway. He wouldn't be good for anyone long term. Or, hell, even short term. And it wouldn't just be Leah soon. There was no way he was inflicting himself on some poor, defenseless kid, but he had to give her some reason.

"I get a great story where I get to be the hero who swoops in and saves the day."

She snorted. "There are easier ways to get a great story."

"True."

"So, what's the real answer?"

He sighed and sat back on the couch. The woman didn't let up. Most people took his answers at face value, laughed like they were supposed to, and left him alone. Five minutes with Leah and he was already sweating bullets.

"I don't know," he said finally. "I get to help a woman I really like. And being married to a fine, upstanding citizen such as yourself wouldn't hurt me in the business department, I guess." He frowned a little. "I'm Cole's equal partner in our company, but if someone wants to have a serious conversation about something, I'm the last person they come to. I'm the class clown."

Her eyebrows rose and he held up a hand. "Yeah, I know, I do what I can to keep that reputation alive and strong. But it might be nice to be taken seriously for once."

She nodded. "Okay, so we do this marriage thing. You help me keep my job. I'll help you look like a responsible adult at yours, and then we go our separate ways."

"Sounds like a plan."

She stuck out her hand for a handshake. He glanced down at it and then back up at her, before moving in closer.

"You know, we did just get engaged. I can think of a few

more appropriate ways to seal the deal."

Her mouth dropped open with a small intake of breath, her eyes zeroing in on his lips.

"I…um…" She shook her head and sat back. "I think we need to set some ground rules."

He frowned at that. Rules sucked. "Such as?"

"No sex."

It was his turn for his mouth to drop open in surprise. "Isn't sex the one big perk of marriage?"

"It's not a real marriage, remember?"

"Doesn't mean we can't have some real sex."

Her lips twitched and he moved in closer, but she didn't take the bait. "Sex complicates things, and this situation is plenty complicated already."

"Well, that's true enough."

She folded her hands in her lap. "So…when do we…I mean when should we…"

He slapped his hands on his knees and stood up, holding his hands out to her. "No time like the present."

• • •

Leah blinked at Brooks, stunned at the speed with which things were moving. Half an hour ago she was moving into her new on-campus quarters, preparing to start her new life at the school, and now she was facing down a fake marriage with a playboy billionaire, who apparently wanted to get married right that second. "What? Now?"

"Sure. Why not? Busy?"

"We can't just go get married right now."

"Why not?"

Good question. Other than it being totally freaking insane, territory they'd already covered. "Don't we have to have a license or something?"

He frowned. "Oh, probably. Hang on."

He pulled out his phone.

"Who are you calling?"

"Cole."

"What?" She jumped up and tried to pull the phone from his hand. "Don't call him. Then he'll know."

That damn eyebrow of his rose again. "People are going to know anyway. Might as well tell a few of them now. Cole, hey," he said into the phone. "Do you need a license to get married, and if so how do I go about getting one?"

She could hear the laughter through the phone and groaned. She was never living this down.

Brooks, bless his crazy little heart, kept trying to convince Cole he was serious. She pulled out her own phone and googled the info, turning the screen so Brooks could see.

"Oh, never mind. Leah found the info." He frowned at the phone. "Damn. Says we have to wait at least twenty-four hours." He glanced at her and she shrugged. "Well, I guess that gives you some notice if you want to come. Leah and I are getting married tomorrow evening. I'll let you know where when we figure it out."

He hung up the phone while Cole was still shouting something unintelligible. Not surprisingly, Kiersten called Leah moments later.

Brooks took her hand. "Ignore it for now. We'll call anyone we want there once we've got the details in place. First, we need to get a license. You ready?"

Her stomach took a roller-coaster trip around her body, sending her head spinning. "Not even a little bit."

He pulled her into his arms and planted a quick kiss on her. That sent her heart rate racing for a whole different reason. It did halt the panic in its tracks, though.

"Stop overthinking this. You need a husband. I'm available. End of story."

"I still think this is a bad idea."

He grinned. "Probably, but sometimes those are the best ones."

She took a deep breath and blew it out slowly, then nodded. "Okay."

Instead of letting her go, he pulled her closer. But this time when he kissed her, there was nothing quick about it. He set about a leisurely exploration of her mouth that had her holding on to him for support. She knew she should push him away. Kissing like that was going to lead to a lot of other things and that had been the one and only rule. No sex. She'd been the one to make the rule. And if he kept kissing her like that, she was going to be the one to toss it right out the window.

But she'd never been kissed so well and so thoroughly in her life. All the damn songs finally made sense. All the cheesy romance novels she'd ever read where the heroine melts in her hero's arms while stars and little cupids float around her head weren't so cheesy anymore. She was melting all right, right into a big puddle of quivering, wanting desire. Some rational part of her brain kept her from climbing him like a high-school gym rope, but just barely.

When he finally released her, her brain floated in a fog of raging hormones that even rational thought couldn't touch.

He stared down at her, his heart pounding against where her fingers lay on his muscled chest. "We are renegotiating the honeymoon terms."

Her brain started screeching *danger, Will Robinson!* But the only response she could muster was a nod. Was it a terrible idea? Oh hell, yes. Did she care? Nope.

Brooks aimed a grin at her that sent every cell in her body into energized overload.

He took her hand. "Come on, wifey. Let's go get hitched," he said, towing her toward the door.

She managed to keep the "hell, yeah" inside and muttered something along the lines of "okay" as she followed him to his car. Even she had to admit, as far as necessary evils went, Brooks Larson might not be such a bad choice. She hoped.

It looked like she was about to find out.

# Chapter Six

The driver opened Leah's door and she looked around the back alley as she climbed out of the car.

"Why are we sneaking in the back door?" she asked Brooks, who chuckled and took her hand, leading her to the door, which opened like magic as they approached.

"If we went in the front door then someone might recognize me and then there'd be cameras and questions, and I assumed you'd prefer a more private shopping experience."

She did, indeed. And the fact that he'd thought of her sent a little tingle of warmth through her body. It didn't, however, ease the riot currently happening in her stomach. Skulking into the back room of a jewelry store for a wedding ring wasn't exactly how she'd envisioned the whole getting engaged thing. Then again, nothing that had happened in the last few months, and certainly the last few days, was anything like she'd ever envisioned. At this point, she needed to stop trying to make sense of anything and just go along for the ride.

They were led into a lavishly decorated private showroom

and seated in gold brocade chairs that probably cost more than she made in a year. She perched on the end, not wanting to crinkle the fabric. Brooks, on the other hand, sprawled into the chair and hooked an ankle over his knee, looking for all the world like he was in his favorite recliner about to watch a game.

A sharply dressed man entered, followed by four employees who reminded Leah of flight attendants. Only these attendants weren't carrying open cans of soda and tiny bags of pretzels. They carried black velvet trays covered in glittering rings.

"All of this isn't necessary," she said, eyeing the huge rocks spread on the tray.

"Of course it is," Brooks said, looking over the selection. "You're my fiancée. People will be taking pictures, and most of those pictures will be zooming in on your left hand. I have a reputation to uphold. I am many things, but cheap isn't one of them." He winked at her. "Besides, there are relatively few perks to marrying me. Might as well get something out of it."

"I've already told you, I don't need or want anything from you." She tried to speak quietly as the store manager was looking at them with a confused and curious expression. As well he should. She was pretty confused herself.

"I don't think that's totally true." He gave her a heated look that shot a raging torrent of desire straight to her core, and brought her hand to his lips, nipping at one of her fingers.

She jumped and yanked her hand away, her cheeks flaming hot.

Brooks sighed. "You don't have to fight me over everything."

She couldn't stop the small grin. "I know."

He smiled back and shook his head. "Just pick something."

She glanced at all the rings, each one easily three carats or more. "Don't you have anything a little smaller?" she asked.

The jeweler looked at Brooks with surprise. "Most ladies prefer to see something larger," he said.

"Oh, she's already seen—"

"Don't say it," she said, jumping in before he could finish the pornographic thought. It might be impossible to instill some sort of public decency in him by sheer willpower, but she'd damn well try.

He grinned at her and then turned back to the jeweler. "She's not most ladies."

Just when she'd reached her bullshit threshold he went and said something sweet. He'd be the death of her.

"Really, a plain wedding band would be fine," she said, hoping to appeal to his chivalrous side. "I'm not trying to be difficult, but it really is what I'd prefer."

Brooks looked like he was going to argue, but instead sighed deeply and turned back to the jeweler.

"Can we see a selection of wedding bands?"

"Of course, sir." The jeweler waved over his assistants. They disappeared through the door and quickly returned, each sporting a new velvet-clad tray.

Leah looked over these with growing dismay. Most of them were nearly as bejeweled as the engagement rings. How could any of them be remotely comfortable to wear? The stones would press into her skin and drive her nuts. Not to mention the fact that she'd be terrified to wear it anywhere without an armed guard. But she did finally see a few bands that were a little less ornate. She chose a thin white gold band set with several round diamonds evenly spaced around the circumference.

"Could we do something like this…only without the diamonds?"

The jeweler looked at Brooks, obviously at a loss for words.

"What if we made the diamonds smaller? Or added some sort of design?" Brooks said. "Like an engraving."

The jeweler nodded, somewhat mollified. "That would be easy enough. Did you have something in mind?"

"Maybe a flowering vine that wraps around the band?"

"I think that would be lovely, sir," the jeweler said, nodding his approval.

Brooks glanced at Leah. "Would that be acceptable?"

She nodded. It sounded quite beautiful, and simple enough not to embarrass her. "It sounds very nice, thank you."

Brooks turned to the jeweler with a smile of triumph. "Well then, I guess that will be all for today. But make it in platinum instead of white gold."

"Excellent, sir." The jeweler jumped up before Leah could protest.

Brooks held up a finger. "Oh, and make mine a matching platinum band without the design, please."

"Why do you get a plain band?" Leah whispered at him.

"Shhh," he said.

The jeweler nodded again, but his affable expression disappeared when Brooks said, "We'll need these by tomorrow afternoon. Actually, morning would be better."

The jeweler's face paled, but he nodded with a forced smile. "Of course, sir. I'll have these ready for you first thing in the morning."

"Wonderful." Brooks stuck out his hand for a handshake and then turned to take Leah's hand to lead her back out the door.

"I'll have to give him a massive tip or buy you a nice wedding present from here," Brooks said. "Compensate him for the time he's going to be spending tonight getting those rings ready."

"If you would have let me get a plain band like I asked it

wouldn't be a problem."

"Maybe I'd like the chance to spoil you a little. It's not like I've ever had a wife before. And I won't have one long. Being a doting husband for a few months could be fun, if you'd let it."

"Only a few months, huh?" she said with half a grin.

"Oh, believe me, after a few months of being shackled to me, you'll be begging the judge to release you."

She could see herself begging for release, but it wouldn't be a judge she'd be pleading with. She glanced at Brooks from the corner of her eye, hoping he didn't notice her sudden flushed cheeks or jumping heart rate. The artery in her neck was probably visibly pulsing. Thinking of Brooks tended to make *everything* pulse.

"Like it or not," Brooks said, waving the driver away and opening the car door for her, "you will soon be Mrs. Brooks Larson. I have a reputation to uphold. You might have to fancy it up every now and then. And since money isn't an issue, you definitely need to take advantage of me. I insist."

She resisted the urge to sigh. She'd known that being his wife, even for a short time and even if it wasn't real, would mean stepping out of her comfort zone.

Brooks slid in beside her, laughing. "I've never met a woman who treated wearing diamonds with such distaste. You'd think I was asking you to wear a ball of slime on your finger."

Her lips twitched. "It's not that bad. It's just not what I'm used to. I wouldn't be comfortable with something that large. Don't say it," she said when his mouth opened again.

"You read my mind far too easily," he said instead.

She laughed. "It's not really hard when your mind seems to permanently reside in the gutter."

"This is probably true."

"As I was saying, wearing a massive diamond on my

finger, especially since I work with children all day, might not be the best idea. I'd be too afraid to lose it."

Brooks looked thoughtful for a minute and then nodded. "I guess I can see that."

It was her turn to show some surprise and he laughed again. "What? I can be reasonable occasionally."

"Good to know. I was starting to wonder."

They drove up the street a short distance to several trendy clothing stores, including the studio of a bridal designer Leah had only seen in magazines.

Brooks jumped out and held the door open for her. Leah looked inside the window to see Kiersten waiting for her.

"You ladies have fun," Brooks said, getting back into the car.

"Oh yeah," she muttered under her breath.

Shopping for a wedding dress she would never be able to afford on her own to marry a man she barely knew so she could fool a nun she'd recently met into thinking she wasn't the Harlot of the Year sounded like heaps of fun. How much did it take for a person to get sent to hell?

Though, despite her misgivings and the sheer craziness of the entire situation, she couldn't help the small flutter of excitement in her belly. Like many little girls, she had always dreamed of what her wedding dress might look like. And while this might not be a real wedding, and it would be more appropriate to wear some simple off-the-rack dress, the thought of trying on gorgeous gowns appealed to her more than she wanted to admit.

She went inside to meet the girls with a much greater bounce in her step than she'd had with the jewelry. With the dress, she could have fun for a day, dress like a princess, and then put it away. A ring would have been a reminder every day of the absurdity of it all.

The dress though... She stared at one of the enormous

confections in the window, her smile growing. She could have a little fun with a dress…as long as she didn't think about the wedding night when her groom would normally be taking it off.

• • •

Kiersten opened the curtain a little so she could pass in another dress. "Here, try this one."

Leah took it and hung it on the little hook until she could unzip the one she was wearing. "This isn't necessary."

"It's absolutely necessary. You're getting married. You need a dress. What were you planning on doing? Heading down to the courthouse in your jeans?"

"No," Leah said, trying on the sixth dress. "I was going to wear a nice dress, one that I already have. Seems kind of pointless to buy a new dress for something like this."

"Something like this? You mean your wedding?"

"But it's not really my wedding. I mean it is, but you know what I mean."

Kiersten laughed. "All I'm saying is you only get a first wedding once. You might as well make the most of it. What does your mom have to say about all this?"

"We didn't have much time to talk about it but she's thrilled I'm getting married. And disappointed she can't come. I wouldn't have told her about it at all, but I didn't want to risk her hearing it from somebody else. I mean Brooks is kind of…well kind of a…"

"Celebrity?" Kiersten said.

"Something like that. The first thing my mom did when I told her was google him. And she wasn't totally thrilled about all the stuff that came up. But I think she's too busy swooning to complain. How in the world did I get mixed up with a guy like him?"

"I know exactly how you feel," Kiersten said. "Hell, when I married Cole he was in *People* magazine's Sexiest Men edition. It's definitely an interesting group to marry into."

"It's not one I should be marrying into. He should be marrying a model or an actress or Miss Universe or someone."

"Here, try this one, too." Kiersten passed in another dress. "I think you're forgetting the fact he's dated all those women before. None of them stuck, and yet you've managed to snag him with hardly even trying."

"What do you mean hardly trying? I haven't tried at all."

"Well, now you're just bragging."

Leah groaned. "You know what I mean. I can't believe this has gone this far. I haven't snagged him. Didn't want to snag him. The only reason we're in this mess is because he couldn't keep his mouth shut in front of my boss."

Kiersten laughed again. "Yeah, keeping his mouth shut isn't one of Brooks's strong suits. Don't get me wrong; he's a great guy. He's just a bit of a goofball is all."

Leah sighed and zipped up another dress. "This is a disaster waiting to happen, even for a temporary marriage. We still have to be roommates for a while. We'll probably kill each other inside of a week."

"It won't be that bad," Kiersten said. "Now come out and let me see that one."

Leah came out and stood in front of the three-panel mirror, turning a little from side to side so she could see all the angles.

"Oh, I love that one," Kiersten said.

"I think I do, too," Leah said, doing one more twist to see the back.

It was a tasteful lace dress with three-quarter-length sleeves that fell in a flaring skirt to her knee. Simple but beautiful. Perfect for a fake shotgun wedding.

"I think that's the one," Kiersten said.

"Agreed." Leah gave her a big smile.

"See? Aren't you glad I made you come dress shopping?"

Leah laughed. "Yes, I guess it will be nice to have something presentable to be married in. Oh, God," she said, burying her face in her hands. "This is insane."

"It is. But sometimes insane works. Look," Kiersten said, prying Leah's hands from her face. "It might be crazy, but it's also about the only thing you can do to save your job, right?"

Leah nodded.

"Well, then, you might as well make the best of it. Brooks is a good guy. He's also drop-dead gorgeous and filthy rich to boot. You've got the winning trifecta right there. No matter what reason you guys are giving for doing this, the fact remains you are going to be married to him in a few hours. So why not enjoy it?"

"That's what he says."

"He is occasionally right," Kiersten said with a grin.

"And if it all blows up in my face?"

"At least you'll get a good story out of it."

Leah laughed. "That part, at least, is true." She took one last glance in the mirror. "Do you think he'll like it?"

Kiersten grinned. "Honey, he's going to love it."

# Chapter Seven

The intercom buzzed and Brooks smiled. He'd hoped his friends would drop by. With Leah out dress shopping, it was the perfect opportunity for a little impromptu bachelor party. He knew he could count on his friends to come through.

He glanced at the computer monitor which showed him the security feed. Harrison, Chris, and Cole stood clustered on the street. He buzzed them in and opened his door.

"What's this?" he asked as they all marched inside.

"You know what it is," Harrison said, handing him a six-pack.

"The girls are out doing their thing," Cole said. "So we're here to have a little fun ourselves."

"Can't let you get married without some sort of a send-off," Chris said. "Fake wedding or not."

"And here I thought you guys had forgotten all about me."

"Ah, mate," Harrison said. "You know we wouldn't do that."

"What's the plan?" Brooks said, cracking open his first

beer.

"Well, with an hour's notice, you're looking at it," Cole said. "Just you, your best friends, a bunch of booze, and a poker table. Couldn't ask for a more perfect night."

There might be room to debate that, but before Brooks could say anything, his intercom buzzed again.

"With a couple extra guests," Chris said.

Brooks's eyebrows hit his hairline. "Please don't tell me you got me strippers."

"Okay, I won't," Chris said with a grin.

Brooks buzzed them in without even looking at the monitor. His hesitation confused him. Normally, he'd be all over the idea. But this time…he wondered if he could politely excuse himself from his own party.

He shook his head, going to the door to open it. "You guys are insane, you know that?" he said.

"And why is that, dear?" a female voice said.

Brooks whirled around. He knew that voice.

"Mom?"

He looked from her to his friends and back again, but they all looked just as stunned as he was.

"Close your mouth, dear. You'll catch flies like that. Are you going to let us in?"

"Us?"

She walked past him and looked at everyone standing there with a drink. "Look, Craig. We got here in time for a party."

Brooks's dad followed her in and nodded at Brooks. "Son," he said. His dad had always been one of few words.

"Well now, what do we have here? We aren't interrupting anything, are we?"

"Kind of," Brooks said. "We have a bit of a bachelor party going on here. I thought you weren't going to be in until tomorrow morning."

"We got in early and decided we'd rather come see you than hang out at a hotel."

"That's great, Mom," Brooks said. "But I'm not sure this is the type of thing you want to hang around for."

"Oh, I don't know. I've always wondered what goes on at these things."

Brooks opened his mouth, but before he could say anything else the door buzzed again.

*Oh God. The strippers.*

"That must be more of your friends," his mom said, walking to the door.

"Wait, Mom..."

But she had already hit the buzzer and gone to open the door.

Brooks looked at his dad, horrified. His dad just raised an eyebrow. Big help.

"Brooks," his mom said in that sickly sweet voice that usually meant he was in a lot of trouble. "Are these ladies friends of yours?"

"Sorry, Mrs. Larson," Chris said. "I asked them to come."

"I see."

Where did moms learn that special tone that made kids cringe? They didn't even have to say anything much to convey a world of disappointment. Two words and four grown-ass men went from jovial partygoers to chastised adolescents, standing in the middle of his apartment, their eyes downcast, as if they'd been caught cheating on an exam or sneaking a dessert before dinner.

"I'm afraid there's been a mistake," she said to the women at the door. "I don't think we will be needing your...services tonight."

Brooks rubbed his hand over his face. Having his mother turn strippers away from his door was definitely going to make his Top 10 List of Embarrassing Moments. It could have been worse, though. She could have shown up mid-show. And as embarrassing as it was to suddenly feel like a hormonal thirteen-year-old being caught by his mother doing something naughty, he had to admit he was a little relieved the strippers were gone. What was the proper response when one's mother got rid of unwanted strippers for you? Thanks, Mom?

She closed the door on them and turned around. "It looks like you're going to need some more entertainment for the night."

"Mom," Brooks said. He laughed, but sudden and horrifying images of his mother trying to entertain his friends flooded his mind. If she broke out Pin the Tail on the Bachelor, he was out of there.

"What? I'm not a total prude. You are entitled to a little fun the night before your wedding, which you only told your mother about a few hours ago."

"A little fun with my mother, for my bachelor party?"

"I realize that has therapy written all over it, but I promise it won't be that bad."

Brooks looked at his father who just shrugged helplessly. His mother grabbed her purse from where she dropped it on the table. "Come on, boys. We passed a bar down the street. Let's all go get a drink. My treat."

They all looked at each other, but none of them were willing to say no to her. So they all shuffled out the door on their way to what had to be the worst bachelor party ever.

Thirty minutes and three drinks later, Brooks knew he'd made a mistake. There were, in fact, quite a few things more humiliating than having a bachelor party thrown by your mother. One of them was having your mother become the life of the party.

She'd failed to mention that the bar she'd seen was a karaoke bar. She'd also failed to mention that she and his father were karaoke aficionados. Three things about that. One, apparently once all the kids left the house, parents will pick up surprising hobbies and, rather than taking up knitting or bowling, his parents liked to hit the bar and belt out a few tunes. Good to know. Two, his mother sang surprisingly well. Her rendition of "Girls Just Wanna Have Fun" damn near brought tears to his eyes. And three, the fact that she was singing that song directly to his father, making come-hither eyes and crooking her finger at him, was going to have him in therapy for a solid five years. Minimum.

The song ended. Everyone clapped. Brooks thought the worst was over.

He was so very, very wrong.

His dad slammed back a shot and clapped him on the shoulder. "Be right back, son. Don't let anyone steal my drink."

Brooks watched him saunter—yes, literally saunter…his quiet, book-loving, nerdy professor father—up to the stage. He took a microphone so he and Brooks's mother could sing a duet.

The first notes of the song filtered out into the crowd and the hand holding his drink suspended midair in total shock. That song wasn't a duet. That song shouldn't be sung as a duet. That song shouldn't be sung period. Not by parents. In public. To each other. While on stage. IN PUBLIC.

He managed to tear his eyes away from his parents singing "I Touch Myself" by the Divinyls long enough to glance at his friends. Yep. Good to know it wasn't just him. Harrison sat in some sort of horrified stupor, his slow blinking the only sign that he was still breathing. Chris had a weird half grin on his face, like he couldn't decide if he was amused or ready to bolt out the door. Cole…

"Put that down!" Brooks said, swatting at the phone in Cole's hand.

Cole laughed and leaned away so he could keep filming. "There is no way in hell I'm putting this phone down." Cole fended him off with one hand and kept recording his parents with the other.

"You have to sleep some time," Brooks said.

"Oh, come on. It's kind of sweet," Cole said.

"Really, *really* not the word that comes to mind," Brooks said, abandoning his phone-snatching attempts in the interest of downing another drink to dull the memory currently being branded into his brain.

"I'm serious," Cole said. He pointed up at the stage. "There are two people who have been married over thirty years, having a blast and hanging all over each other. I know people who have been together for thirty days who aren't as into each other as your parents are. Relationship goals, man."

Brooks risked another glance at the stage where the song had thankfully just ended. And his father celebrated by giving his mother a kiss that had the crowd roaring their approval. On the one hand, the little boy in him wanted to vomit in the corner. And would do so shortly, for more than one reason. But on the other...okay, he could see Cole's point.

His parents made their way back to the table and his dad grabbed his beer, taking a large swig, while his mom grabbed her purse.

"I'm going to freshen up."

His dad leaned over and smacked her right on the ass. "Hurry back."

Brooks took the beer out of his hand. "I'm cutting you off."

His dad just grinned at him. "Sorry, your mother's still got it."

"Oh my God. Dad."

His dad shrugged. "Son, my dearest hope for you is that you'll be sitting at some table in some bar thirty years from now impatiently waiting for your wife to come back from the restroom so you can drag her back to your hotel room."

"Dad!" He wondered if his therapist's number was in his wallet. He really needed to start carrying that card around.

"Look," his dad said, his face returning to its usual serious expression. "I don't know everything that's going on with you, and frankly I don't need to. You're a grown man, you can make your own decisions. I just hope that the girl you're marrying tomorrow is one you can see yourself still drooling over a few decades from now. Now, if you'll excuse me," he said, pushing back from the table as his wife rejoined them, "we'll see you boys at the courthouse tomorrow."

Brooks's mom leaned down to kiss his forehead and then giggled as his dad grabbed her hand and hauled her toward the door.

Cole raised a drink in their direction. "Like I said, relationship goals."

Brooks watched them go, his mind warring between wanting to be bleached until all remaining memories of the last hour had been scrubbed from it permanently, and wanting to burn every second into his synapses so he could have some sort of perfect marriage blueprint to follow.

Not that he and Leah were going to have a real marriage. But maybe, for someday. If he ever found anyone else he wanted to marry. Though he couldn't see that happening. He wasn't a marriage kind of guy—said the guy sitting at his bachelor party. But he wasn't a *real* marriage kind of guy.

Then again, maybe he just hadn't found the kind of girl who made him want to be one.

The sudden image of Leah smiling at him with a come-hither look had him knocking back another drink.

What was he getting himself into?

# Chapter Eight

Brooks stood with Leah in front of a guy in a courthouse and repeated vows he had no intention of keeping.

Well, that wasn't totally true. He'd keep them for a while. Maybe it was more accurate to say he had no intention of keeping them permanently. Cole handed him a ring and he slipped it on Leah's finger. Her hand trembled slightly in his, and a wave of tenderness washed over him. Okay, if he was ever tempted to do the whole marriage thing for real, Leah would be the one to tempt him. He gave her hand a squeeze and she rewarded him with a shy smile as she slipped on his own ring.

He still wanted to find a way to get her a big, fat rock. Once the marriage was dissolved she could sell it. Stash away a nice little nest egg. An easy and unobtrusive way of getting some money into her pocket without handing her a wad of cash since she kept flat-out refusing that, too. What ex-wife didn't want alimony? He needed to get the stubborn woman to stop refusing everything.

Not that it should matter. The wedding was fake. The

relationship was fake. But Leah in that white dress…very, very real. In fact, the more they continued, the more real everything felt.

He'd been half convinced he should call it off until the moment Leah had walked into the room. There were other ways to deal with her problems. If she was too stubborn to take his money outright—and judging by the way she insisted they sign the ironclad prenup Cole had drawn up stating she got nothing no matter why the marriage ended, he was sure he wouldn't be able to convince her to take it any other way—then he could always find her a job. Set up anonymous donations or scholarships for the kid. Enlist Kiersten's help in making the woman see reason.

But then she'd walked into that courthouse room, in a white lacy dress that floated around her knees, her hair pulled back with a simple silver headband that left her brunette waves free to fall to her shoulders, and he'd shut down any other thought in his head but making her his. It wouldn't be forever. It *shouldn't* be forever, for her sake. But for a little while he could pretend that a woman like her would marry a man like him under circumstances other than extreme duress with her fingers crossed behind her back.

"You may kiss your bride."

All other thoughts evaporated. This was the part of the ceremony he'd been looking forward to. She didn't seem nearly as eager, glancing around at their friends who'd been able to make it to a last-minute wedding with a bright blush staining her cheeks. He took her chin in his hands and drew her gaze back to him. She smiled and his heart exploded. He barely knew this woman and he'd willingly lay the world at her feet for one more of those smiles.

He leaned down and placed a soft kiss on her lips, reining in the urge to do much, much more. It would embarrass her and the day was hard enough for her as it was. But later, when they were alone…they still needed to renegotiate some terms. It was their wedding night after all.

"Congratulations," the officiant said. He handed them some paperwork and looked behind them for the next couple who waited their turn.

Kiersten gave him a quick hug, standing on her tiptoes to whisper in his ear. "I realize this isn't supposed to be real, but there is obviously something going on between you two. If you hurt her…"

"That is the last thing I intend to do," he said.

"Good." She dropped back down and smiled up at him. "Well then…" She wrapped her arm around Leah and led her out while Cole clapped him on the shoulder.

"You just won me a ton of money," he said with a grin.

Brooks raised an eyebrow. "And how did I do that? More importantly, where's my share?"

Cole chuckled and nodded back at Harrison and Chris who were pulling up the rear. "Harrison bet that you'd never go through with it."

"You bet I would?" Brooks snorted. "I'd have bet with Harrison."

"Naw. I have a feeling about you two." He nodded up at Leah who was climbing into the limo behind Kiersten.

"Don't go getting all attached," Brooks said. "This is only temporary."

Cole nodded, a smug smile of monogamous wisdom plastered to his face that had Brooks itching to knock it off.

"Oh, before I forget," Cole said. "Here. The boys and I got you a wedding present."

He slapped a string of condoms into Brooks's hand. "Probably not necessary, I know, but hey, we have high hopes for you, buddy."

"You guys are dicks."

"Yeah, that's why you love us."

“Nothing is happening tonight. The last thing we want is to complicate an already complicated relationship.”

“Why? You might enjoy being married.”

“Not everyone is cut out for marriage, you know.”

Cole laughed outright at that. “Says the guy who just got married.”

“That’s…it’s not…shut up.”

He jumped into the car before Cole could say anything else.

The dinner their friends graciously treated them to seemed never-ending. He appreciated the gesture, but the whole situation was weird. Celebrating something that had literally been set up to be broken. But hey, free dinner. No complaints on his part. His eyes, though, strayed often to Leah. Better yet, her eyes strayed often to him.

By the end of dinner, he felt like they’d been playing footsy all night, only it wasn’t nearly as satisfying as the real thing because they’d never actually touched each other. And he wanted to touch her more than he’d ever wanted anything. That was saying something. He was a greedy guy. There were a lot of things he wanted.

And he’d give them all for one night with her.

# Chapter Nine

Leah stood beneath the hot water of the hotel shower, letting the jets massage the ache from her scalp.

How a somewhat impromptu fake-ish wedding had turned into such an affair, she had no idea. Well, that wasn't totally true. She was now married to a billionaire. Who was friends with billionaires. Who liked to party like billionaires. Whereas she would have done a quick courthouse wedding and a nice dinner at a Sizzler somewhere, they'd paid a fortune for the nicest restaurant in town, dropped enough on dinner to pay her rent for several months, and still felt like they'd gotten off cheap.

She wasn't complaining. The night had been memorably beautiful, and fake or not, she appreciated having a nice wedding. Hell, it might be the only one she ever got. It was just...different, that's all. She didn't know if she'd ever get used to it.

Her wedding ring brushed across her bare skin and she looked down at it. Another thing she'd never get used to. She was married now. A "Mrs." She could have a whole new name if she wanted it. In fact, her employers would expect a name change. The thought unsettled her, like she was suddenly supposed to be this whole other person because she'd said "I do" to some guy she barely knew.

She almost had to laugh at herself. She was having a baby with a man she barely knew and was newly married to a different man she barely knew. Her mother would be so proud. She completely blocked out any thought of how that conversation was going to go down. She'd deal with it later. Right now, she had to walk out into that massive hotel suite and say good night to her husband.

Not how she pictured her wedding night going, especially when she was married to a man like Brooks.

She'd known extremely good-looking men before. Not just handsome men, but Chris Hemsworth, Jason Momoa, over-the-top hot men. And many of them had a bit of a cocky swagger about them that let the world know they knew exactly how hot they were. But Brooks didn't have that. Oh, he joked about how hot he was. The man was a master flirt, but something about the way he said it made her think that deep down inside, he didn't believe a word of what came out of his mouth.

The water flowed over her in hot rivulets, sending tingling sparks through her over-sensitized body. She seemed to experience everything at a heightened level lately. Smells, sounds…touch. She let her hands trail down her body, sucking in a breath at the sensations that rippled down.

A knock at the door startled her and she turned off the water, embarrassed, though he had no idea what she'd been doing, and probably would have loved every second if he had.

"Everything okay in there?" he asked.

"Yes," she said, stepping out and grabbing a towel. She bent over to flip her hair upside down and towel-dried it for a second before wrapping it up. "Give me a moment."

The door opened and she squealed, whipping her hair towel down to cover her body, though the tiny towel didn't cover much.

"I'm sorry. I thought you said come in."

"I said *give me a moment*."

"Sorry," he said again. "I'll just wait out there."

He jerked his thumb toward the door, but didn't make any move to follow it. He stood still, his gaze roaming over her body, sucking in a deep breath as he took in every inch of her.

She should scream, push him away, give him a good chewing out for standing there staring at her.

Instead, she returned the favor. She couldn't help it. He only wore plaid pajama bottoms, slung low on his hips. His broad chest and shoulders were on spectacular display and he sported a tribal band tattoo around one impressive bicep that both surprised her and made her clench her fists in her towel to keep from reaching out and tracing it with her fingertips.

His height showed in his long torso and legs. She'd never wanted a pair of pants to fall off so badly in her life. Even his bare feet were unexpectedly erotic.

"I think I should go," he said, his voice hoarse. He turned half away but didn't take his eyes off her.

Twisting like that gave her an excellent view of his rock-hard ass, though, and she bit her lip. Holy hell.

Screw it. Seriously. It was a bad idea that she was pretty sure she'd regret in the morning. But she wanted him. Craved him. Wanted to feel his touch so badly she was seconds from sobbing from her need and desire. And this man, this gloriously incredible man, was theoretically, *legally*, hers.

"Brooks," she said, her own voice sounding hoarse with need to her own ears. "Don't go."

He sucked in a breath, his hungry eyes moving over her again. "One of us needs to walk away right now. If I stay—"

"Brooks," she said again.

Then she dropped her towel.

• • •

Brooks's brain short-circuited. Every precaution, every warning, every rational thought completely and totally evaporated on a wave of lust so strong he nearly dropped to his knees at the feet of the goddess who stood before him.

He walked slowly toward her, giving her time to change her mind. When he stood within a breath's distance of her, he paused again, closed his eyes and breathed her in.

Her hands came up and rested on his waist and that was it. His control disintegrated.

He cupped her face, turning her lips up to meet his. She clung to him as he plundered her mouth. All that creamy, smooth skin pressed against him and he wrapped his arms around her, trying to bring her even closer. Finally, he picked her up, groaning against her lips when her legs wrapped around his waist. Shit, she wasn't even trying to do anything but hang on and he was seconds from blowing.

He carried her out of the bathroom and straight to the bed. He laid her down and got rid of his pants. She sucked in a breath at the sight of him and he gave her a moment to look. Only fair since he'd certainly had a chance to admire every line and curve of her gorgeous body.

The sheer beauty of her stunned him. Humbled him. And she was *his*. His wife.

The knowledge of that did something to him, gave him a sense of both possession and pride that he'd never felt before.

He belonged. He was a part of a *we*. An *us*.

The intimacy in that tiny word rocked him.

It didn't matter if it was temporary. For that moment, they belonged to each other, and each other only.

When he finally climbed up next to her, she reached for him eagerly. Fingers threading through his hair, guiding him to her lips. He kissed her with growing urgency, and she was right there with him, kissing him like he'd never been kissed before. With total abandon, every stroke of her tongue branding him more deeply as hers.

His body begged for more, ached for more. He couldn't get enough.

His hands trailed over her body, closing over a breast, hesitating when she flinched away from his touch.

"Sorry," she said. "They're a bit sore."

"No apologies. Just tell me if something doesn't feel good, and tell me what does."

He ran his fingertips lightly over her breast, barely skimming over the skin, watching her carefully for her reaction. Her mouth dropped open and he smiled. He longed to suck her tight nipples into his mouth. Instead, he lightly flicked the tip of his tongue over their peaks and she nearly came off the bed.

After that, it became a game to see how lightly he could caress, kiss, and lick her. Her sensitive skin responded to his lightest touch and he had her coming apart in his arms within minutes.

His fingers brushed down her side, down her hips. Then lightly tickled her center. Her hips came off the bed, wanting, *begging.*

He chuckled, then dipped down to recapture her mouth, slipping his tongue between her lips at the same moment that he sank a gentle finger inside her. She gasped, and then the game was over.

She arched against him, straining to drive him deeper, and he was a goner.

He quickly rolled over and grabbed his pants from the floor where he'd dropped them earlier, silently thanking his asshole friends for their perverse sense of humor. He tore a condom from the rest of the pack and had it rolled on before he'd stopped to consider the fact that she was already pregnant, though the condom might still make her more comfortable seeing as they'd pretty much just met.

His hand rested on her belly, another thought invading.

"Is it okay if we…?"

"Absolutely," she said, reaching for him.

"It won't hurt you or…" His fingers stroked across her gently rounded belly and she bit her lip, sucking in a sharp breath.

"The only thing that will hurt me is if you keep torturing me."

"Torture, hmm?" He dipped his head and ran his tongue across the full length of her center, his tongue dipping inside.

She cried out and arched her hips against him. He didn't let up, but he kept his touch light with feather kisses and licks that barely skimmed the surface.

She threw her head back. "Brooks, please," she gasped, and the sound of his name being torn from her lips shattered him into a million pieces.

He slowly sank into her, giving her time to tell him to stop, time to tell him if he was hurting her. She only opened herself wider, pressing into him to draw him in deeper. Her eyes met his as she claimed every inch of him. His body shook with the need to claim her. He tried to set a slow rhythm, but it was too late for that. They both were past that point. He'd make slow, leisurely love to her later. Neither one of them had the patience to wait any longer.

Within a few strokes, she shuddered, the deep heat of her gripping him, bringing her with him, destroying him and saving him all at once. Their gazes locked and the intimacy of that moment seared into his memory. He'd never be free of her now.

He rested beside her for a moment, waiting to regain his equilibrium before he quickly cleaned up. Then he wrapped himself around her, cupping the back of her head to give her a deep, lingering kiss.

She cuddled against him and almost immediately fell asleep. But he stayed awake for a long time afterward, just watching her, holding her, praying to God they both emerged without too much damage.

After what had just happened, there was no way they'd escape unscathed.

# Chapter Ten

A sharp cramp woke Leah and she stirred restlessly, grimacing.

She rolled over, jolting fully awake when she realized she wasn't alone. It took her a moment to remember where she was, and whose arms were around her. But her confusion was quickly replaced by panic when another cramp gripped her belly.

"Brooks," she whispered. He didn't wake. "Brooks," she said again, a little more loudly this time while tapping his arm. He stirred and rolled over with a sleepy grunt.

"Wake up!" She shook his shoulder. "Something's wrong."

He sat bolt upright at that, instantly awake. "What?" he asked. "What is it?"

"I'm not sure. I think there's something wrong with the baby."

His eyes widened with the same panic that coursed through her veins. Her head pounded in time to her furious heartbeat.

"What do you mean?" he asked. "What's the matter?"

"I don't know. My stomach is cramping. I don't think it should be doing that."

"Okay. It's okay." He pulled her to him and kissed her forehead. "We'll get you to the hospital and get you checked."

She placed a hand on her belly. The cramping had stopped. For the moment. Maybe it was nothing. "Wait. I think it's stopped." She took a deep breath. "Maybe it's fine."

Brooks shook his head. "It's not fine if it woke you up from a dead sleep. And even if it is, it won't hurt to get checked out."

She knew he was right, but she didn't want to cause a fuss over nothing. He was already up and pulling on clothes before she swung her legs out of bed. Then she looked down and a wave of dread washed over her. She gasped, tears rushing to her eyes.

Brooks was immediately by her side. "Shit, Leah, you're as white as a sheet."

"Look," she whispered, pointing at a bloodstain the size of a grapefruit on the sheets.

"Oh my God," he said. "Come here, sit down." He led her to a chair.

"I'll mess it up," she said, pulling away.

"I don't care, it doesn't matter. Sit down, please."

He finished throwing on his clothes and brought her a pair of sweatpants from his drawer. "It's okay. Don't worry. We'll get help. I'll call an ambulance."

"I don't need an ambulance. A car is fine."

"But—"

"Brooks," she said, laying a hand on his arm. "If I'm losing the baby, there won't be much they can do to help. If I'm not...a car will get us there fast enough. And I'll feel more comfortable than being hauled out of here on a gurney."

He stared at her for a moment, his eyes wide. Finally,

he nodded and handed her the clothes. Then he grabbed his phone to order a car. She started walking toward the door, but he stopped her, swinging her up and into his arms.

"I can walk," she said.

"I'm sure you can. That doesn't mean you should. And until I know what's wrong with you, I'm not putting you down."

He carried her to the elevator that led out of his apartment and straight to the waiting car. His driver held the door open for them and then rushed around to the driver's seat.

"Get us there in under ten minutes and there's an extra Christmas bonus in it for you."

"Not necessary, sir," his driver said. "I'll get you there." They shot out of the parking garage before Leah could say a word.

Brooks was on his phone texting and making calls to Kiersten and Cole and the doctor at the hospital the whole time, though he would lean over every few minutes to make sure she was doing okay.

"I'm fine. Don't call my mother. I'll call her later once we know what's going on."

Brooks didn't look like he approved, but he didn't argue with her.

Her belly still cramped off and on, but it wasn't the sharp scary pain that had first woken her. Now it was more like a dull ache. Still something she probably shouldn't be feeling, but at least it wasn't horribly painful. That had to be good, right?

When they got to the hospital they were met at the door by two nurses with a wheelchair. Brooks helped her out and into the chair where he took over, waving the nurses ahead to show him the way. Brooks glared when they stopped.

"I'll need these filled out," the nurse behind the counter said.

He grabbed the clipboard she handed him. "Later. I want her in a room now. Where's the doctor?"

"He's coming, sir," the nurse said. "Please be patient."

"I'm not going to be patient," he said in a tone of voice Leah had never heard from him before. He was serious, with a deadly calm that was probably barely containing the explosion beneath, if the white knuckles gripping the handles of her wheelchair were any indication.

"My wife is pregnant and bleeding so we need a doctor now. Get us to her room so I can get her out of this damn chair and into a bed."

"Sir, they are getting her room ready, but we need to have the admission and insurance paperwork filled out…"

Brooks opened his mouth to let loose but Leah grabbed his hand. "Brooks," she said, silently pleading with him to chill out. The fact that he was completely losing his shit for her filled her heart to overflowing. But she needed him to calm down because having a drag-out fight with the nurse who was trying to check them in was going to send Leah straight to the ER.

Luckily for everyone, the doctor, who was apparently a friend of Brooks's, came around the corner.

"Brooks, hi. Sorry, was with another patient. What seems to be the problem?"

Brooks breathed an audible sigh of relief. "Greg, this is my wife. She's pregnant, about fourteen weeks along, and she woke up cramping and bleeding."

"Don't panic. We'll get her settled and see what's going on. Hi, Mrs. Larson," he said, leaning down to shake Leah's hand. She took it gratefully, glad to have him there. Now that the doctor was in front of her, her self-imposed calm denial was beginning to wear off. "Follow me."

The doctor waved them down a corridor. Brooks gave the nurse a parting glare and followed the doctor and nurses down the hallway to where they had set up a private room for Leah. She glanced around as a nurse helped her into a gown and assisted her into bed. She hadn't been to many hospitals before, but the ones she had been to hadn't been nearly as nice. Then again, maybe there'd always been rooms like this, she had just never been with someone important enough to gain access to one. Seriously, the place was nicer than her apartment. She climbed into the bed, biting her lip against another cramp.

Brooks was at her side immediately. "Are you okay?" he asked, leaning down to whisper into her ear.

"I don't know," she said, hating the fear in her voice. She couldn't help it, though. Yes, the pregnancy had been a complete surprise and she'd be lying if she said she hadn't thought at least once that life might be easier if she just miscarried. But she hadn't meant it. And now that the baby was in danger she knew there was nothing she wanted more than to make sure everything was okay.

The doctor spoke with Brooks quietly in the corner and then came over to examine her. "Let's take a look," he said.

He asked her several questions about how she felt and what had happened, along with a few more embarrassing questions about their activities that night while he examined her. Brooks, thankfully, stayed up near her head, holding her hand through the whole thing.

Then the doctor patted her leg. "It looks like the bleeding has stopped, which is a good sign. We're going to do an ultrasound to make sure everything is okay."

She nodded, but glanced up at Brooks. For the first time since she met him, he gave her a smile that didn't reach his eyes. He leaned down to kiss her on the forehead. "It'll be okay," he said, giving her hand a squeeze.

He stood by her side while the doctor squirted the cold gel on her belly and moved the wand around.

After what seemed like an eternity, the fast staccato of her baby's heartbeat filled the room.

"There we are," he said.

Leah's heart clenched and she looked at the monitor where a small black blob quickly beat inside the tiny body of her baby.

"Is that it?" Brooks asked. "That's the baby?"

"Yes," the doctor said. "And everything looks fine. The heart rate is 164 beats per minute. Perfectly normal. Baby is measuring about fourteen weeks along. Is that correct?"

"Yes," Leah said past the lump in her throat. "Are you sure everything is okay? Why would I be bleeding?"

"Well," the doctor said, putting away his equipment, "sometimes that can happen after certain strenuous activities. Especially sexual intercourse."

Leah blushed fifty shades of red, she was sure.

"It's our wedding night," Brooks said.

The doctor nodded. "Ah. Well. For the time being, we might want to put a hold on the honeymoon, along with any other strenuous activities, just to be on the safe side."

The heat rushed to Leah's cheeks and she glanced up at Brooks, but he had his attention fixed on the doctor.

"I want you to come back in the morning so we can take another look and we'll go from there. But as far as I can tell everything looks like it's going to be fine."

Brooks nodded. "Is there anything else we need to do? Does she need to take it easy? Stay in bed?"

"If everything still looks well after tomorrow, she should be fine to go about her normal activities, but take it easy overall."

"Thank you, doctor," Leah said, trying to pour all the gratitude she felt into a handshake.

The doctor nodded and shook Brooks's hand as well. "Just talk to the nurse on the way out. She'll schedule you an appointment."

He left them so she could get dressed.

"Are you sure you're feeling okay?" Brooks asked. "Because I can get him back in here. Or if you'd feel better staying here for the night, I can arrange that. We can stay as long as you'd like."

She smiled at him. "It's not a hotel, we can't just stay."

"Sure we can. I'll buy the damn place if I have to. If you'd feel better staying here, you give me the word."

It took a second for Leah to realize that Brooks was totally serious and capable of doing exactly what he said. To have that kind of pull at her beck and call was both overwhelming and incredibly nice. She would have to be careful not to misuse that kind of power…and not get too used to it.

"I'm doing fine. The cramping has stopped and I don't think I'm bleeding anymore. Do you think the doctor is right? Do you think everything is fine? He's not just saying that?"

"He's the best doctor I know," Brooks said. "I went to college with him in his pre-med years. Never saw the guy drink or go to a party once. All he did was sit around and study."

She smiled at him. "Well, that's definitely the kind of doc I need on my side then."

He gave her another faint smile and then said, "I'll be right back. I'm going to go fill out these papers."

Leah nodded and waited for him to leave before she sat back on the bed with a deep sigh. She put her hand on her belly. "You gave me a scare," she said. "You stay put, little peanut."

She pulled out her phone and sent a quick text to Kiersten. She had no intention of overdoing it, but she did have a lot of things to do. School would be starting in a few weeks and though she hadn't gotten the full tour of Brooks's apartment yet, it was obvious she needed to get a few things.

Starting with food. The kitchen looked like it had never been used. And as a pregnant woman, even with morning sickness, having a plentiful supply of food around had become incredibly important to her. She was either throwing up or starving to death. There didn't seem to be any in-between.

Brooks came back with an armful of flowers and she smiled up at him. "Where on earth did you get those?"

"The gift shop," he said.

She laughed again. "What did you do, buy out the whole place?"

"Kind of. Too much?"

The uncertain hopefulness on his face was almost too much for her to handle. How did men do that? Go from masters of the universe, ordering around everyone in their path, to hopeful little boys that tugged on the heart strings so easily? Total double whammy. Completely unfair.

"Not too much, at all. They're beautiful, Brooks." She took them from him, burying her face in their petals to inhale deeply. "You didn't need to, though."

"I wanted to. They aren't nearly as beautiful as you, but I hoped they'd make you smile."

She was smiling before he finished talking. He looked at her like he wasn't sure what to do. "You're sure you're feeling okay? You don't want to stay?"

"No, no. I'm fine. I'd rather go home now. Maybe take a shower and get some more sleep."

Funny that she already called his place home when she'd only been there a few hours.

"Okay. I've got the car waiting."

He took her elbow and helped her get settled back into the wheelchair.

"I don't know why they make us use these things. I'm capable of walking out on my own."

"Hush," he said, pushing her down the hallway. "It's the

hospital rules. And this is a rule I agree with."

"You wouldn't agree if you were the one getting wheeled out the door."

He chuckled and her heart jumped to hear the sound again. "True, but I'm not the one getting wheeled. You are. And you heard the doctor. He said you have to take it easy and I'm going to be around to make sure you do."

Well, that sounded ominous. "Actually, he said I could resume my normal activities, within reason."

"I've seen your to-do list and it's not remotely reasonable. Not going to happen."

"I'm not going to lie around the house all day. I have school to get ready for and we need to go shopping or we're going to starve to death."

He glanced at her, his eyes wide with surprise. "How do you know I don't have anything in my fridge?"

"I'm pretty sure it still has the factory plastic wrapped around it."

"It does not. I put a new case of beer in there last week."

"Uh-huh," she said. "And is there anything else in there?"

He didn't answer.

She grinned. "I rest my case. We need to go shopping."

"I do have a housekeeper, you know. I can send her out with a shopping list tomorrow."

"Or we could go ourselves like normal people."

Brooks was already shaking his head. "I'm not going to have you traipsing around stores all over town when you're supposed to be taking it easy."

"Did you just say traipsing? I've never traipsed in my life."

He glared down at her. "You know what I mean. Make a list of things you want and I'll have my housekeeper get them for you."

Leah sighed, too tired to change his bullheaded mind at

the moment. He helped her back into the car and wrapped his arm around her when he got in beside her.

She laid her head on his shoulder. "I'm glad you were with me."

He held her tighter. "Me, too. Though I don't think I was much help."

"Are you kidding? You were wonderful. I probably would have stayed home, not wanting to cause a fuss."

"That's the dumbest thing I've ever heard. You can cause as many fusses as you want."

She laughed. "I'll remember that."

"Why do I think that's going to come back to bite me in the ass?"

"Because you're a smart man."

"You know, you may be the first person who's ever said that to me."

This time she looked at him with surprise. "Really? You're the partner and co-founder of one of the biggest development firms in the city."

"Yes, but when Cole Harrington is your partner people tend to not notice that there is anyone else in the room."

She looked at him for a moment, surprised at the trace of hurt she heard in his voice. He was always so busy making everyone laugh that it had never occurred to her that there might be other emotions lurking below the surface. And maybe that's exactly the way he wanted it. She hadn't been with him long and she was already discovering aspects of his character that she never would have guessed.

When they reached home, he settled her on the couch. "Rest here. I'll be right back in a minute."

She lay back against the cushions and he sprinted upstairs. He crashed around a bit in the bedroom, wrestling with something, but she didn't really think about what he might be doing until he came back to get her. He scooped her up in his arms again.

"This is getting ridiculous. I can walk."

"And as I said, just because you can doesn't mean you should. Besides, I like carrying you."

He brought her into the bedroom and laid her on the freshly changed sheets.

"You changed the sheets yourself?" she asked.

"Why do you sound so surprised?"

"I don't know. I guess I never thought of you as a sheet-changing type of guy. Don't you have people waiting in the wings to do that?"

He rolled his eyes at her. "I am capable of taking care of myself. Just because I choose not to doesn't mean I can't. I didn't always have money, you know."

"I didn't know that."

"Cole and I were regular kids until we developed our first app in college. I can do all kinds of things that would probably surprise you."

"Really? Like what?"

"Well, in addition to my awesome bed-making skills, I can also do the laundry, cook, clean a toilet—"

"You clean toilets?"

"I didn't say I enjoy doing it, or that I did it often. I said I was capable of it."

She laughed again. "I might have you clean a few toilets for me to prove that. But let me get my camera first."

He settled her into the bed and pulled the covers up to her chest. "I think right now it's more important you get some rest. We'll talk toilets in the morning."

"Deal," she said.

He stood up and went to leave the room.

"Where are you going?"

"I thought I would sleep on the couch so you could get some more rest."

"I can sleep with you next to me."

"I didn't want to disturb you."

"You won't disturb me, Brooks."

His forehead creased in a worried frown. "I don't want to hurt the baby. The last time I was in bed with you…"

She stared at him for a second, waiting until she had her emotions under control before she spoke. "I get what you're feeling, maybe even more than you do. But you heard the doctor. I'm fine. The baby is fine. We can't have sex at the moment, but we can sleep together. And to be honest, I don't want to be alone. I want to be held. So please, come to bed and hold me."

He stared at her a moment longer and then nodded. "If you're sure it won't disturb you."

"I promise," she said. "It will make me feel safer."

His eyes widened a bit at that.

"Yeah, it surprises me, too," she said with a smile.

He smiled and climbed into bed beside her, though he kept his distance. She wasn't going to let him get away with that, though. She wiggled back against him until she was spooned up against his chest. It took him a few more seconds, but then he wrapped his arm around her and held her close.

"Let me know if you need more space."

"I will," she said, though she had no intention of ever saying a word.

They lay quietly together for a few minutes.

"Brooks?"

"Hmm?" he whispered sleepily.

"I'm glad you were there tonight."

"I'll always be there," he said.

Her heart beat a little quicker at that but she didn't say anything, just wrapped her arm around his and snuggled back against him.

Never in a million years would she have thought that

Brooks Larson would be the type of man she'd want with her in a crisis. But he had kept her calm and gotten her the help she needed when she wouldn't have done it for herself. She had never felt safer and cherished than she did right in that moment.

If this is what a fake marriage to him was like she couldn't begin to imagine what a real one would be like. She cut off that line of thought as soon as it started. There wasn't going to be a real marriage. He might have started out in a middle-class life, but he was living in the stratosphere now and she had no place there. She was a school teacher and was perfectly content to be so. She could never be the socialite wife that he needed despite what he said, but she would play her part for the moment, do what she could to help him, and then they could both go their separate ways.

But for right now, she would enjoy sleeping in his arms. She drifted off to sleep more content than she'd ever been in her life.

# Chapter Eleven

Brooks sat on the back of the couch watching as Leah wandered from one corner of his apartment to the other. With the big loft-style space he could see everywhere she went, for the most part.

He found himself watching her face for signs of things that she liked or disliked. It didn't matter much since she wasn't going to be there long, but he couldn't help but hope that she liked his home.

Of course, it was the ultimate bachelor pad, not really decorated with a woman in mind. To impress one, maybe, but not encourage her to stay. The entire space was framed out in an upscale industrial motif with lots of exposed brick and piping, stark leather furniture, and glass and metal fixtures. He didn't typically bring women back to his apartment. When he wanted to wine and dine them he took them to fancy hotels. If he really wanted to impress them he took them to fancy hotels in Paris or Italy.

His home, though, was his sanctuary away from everyone and everything else. That he'd invited a woman he wasn't even dating to stay there blew his mind. He couldn't process her brand-new wife status at all. That was a mind-fuck of epic proportions. As was her wandering around his apartment looking at his belongings because she would be living among them. Surreal, to be sure.

Of course, that wasn't the only reason he watched her like a hawk. It had been a week since their wedding night when she woke up bleeding. She'd been back to the doctor twice and was cleared to return to her normal life. Sex was still banned for a few weeks, not that he would have touched her anyway. Oh, he still wanted to. So desperately it sent a rush of embarrassment through him every time he thought of it. But the chance that what had happened the last time might happen again terrified him to no end, which was going to make living with her even more interesting. And difficult. But he'd have to power through because he wasn't letting her out of his sight.

"You don't have to keep watching me," she said.

He glanced up and met her gaze. She gave him a soft smile that sent the warm and fuzzies ricocheting around his body. No one else had ever had that effect on him before. The fact that she could do it with a smile alone frightened him a bit—and he loved every second of it.

"I'm not going to break," she said. "The doctor said I was fine."

"I know. I'm making sure you don't steal anything while you're casing my joint."

She laughed and the sound brought a smile to his lips, as it always did.

"So what do you think?" he said when she hadn't made any comments.

"Very nice."

"Just nice?"

"You have a beautiful home, Brooks. It's not exactly to my taste and it could definitely use a woman's touch," she said with a smile, "but it's impressive."

He gave her an exaggerated scowl. "This place is perfect. What are you talking about?"

"It's completely perfect for a permanent bachelor. But I might change a few things if I was moving in for real."

He folded his arms. "Okay, you've piqued my curiosity. What changes would you make?"

She shrugged. "Nothing too drastic. A few pillows. Maybe. Or some curtains," she said, gesturing to the windows that were for the most part bare.

Each floor-to-ceiling window did have a barn-style door hanging to the side of it, except instead of wood it was a hanging sheet of metal that could slide across the window if he wanted to block out the light. It worked wonderfully. Not only did it completely darken the room when he wanted it, but when it was open it served as wall décor. Curtains would ruin the whole aesthetic.

"As I said, it's a beautiful apartment and I can appreciate it for the style that it is. It's just not to my particular taste."

"So what would be your particular taste? Aside from me," he said, running a hand across his chest. She laughed, but her eyes followed the trail he made, and continued checking him out until she realized he was watching her. Her cheeks flashed red and she turned, shrugging like she hadn't just been caught ogling.

"I like warm woods and earth tones. I guess I'm more of a traditional girl."

"What? Like two-story house, picket fence, manicured yard in the suburbs?"

She smiled. "Something like that."

"Really? You don't want to stay in the city?"

"I don't know. I've never given it much thought. I assumed someday when I was married and having kids I would move to a more kid-friendly area."

"People raise kids in the city all the time."

"I know," she said, her hand straying to her belly. "And I will be, too. Plans change, I guess."

Her bright smile seemed a little forced. She sat down on the couch and grabbed a pad of paper that she'd been scribbling on, jotting a few more items on it.

"I have a few things I need to do, so if you need to get back to the office you are more than free to leave me to my own devices. I'll be perfectly fine."

Brooks blinked at that. He hadn't been to the office since their impromptu wedding and he had no plans on returning anytime soon. Things would move along fine without him for a little while, and Cole knew how to get ahold of him if he was needed. He had no intention of leaving Leah on her own.

"I don't have any pressing plans," he said. "And anything you need I can send out for."

"Brooks," she said in that same tone of voice his mom would use when she was trying to get him to understand something he wasn't quite grasping. "The doctor said I am fine. I feel great. Even the morning sickness has almost disappeared. I'm strong and healthy, and feel better than I have in weeks, and I have a class to get ready for. I need to get supplies. I need to get my classroom set up and I would like to pick things out for myself, not send some employee out to get them. I have a lot of things to do. I can't sit around in this apartment all day staring at your face."

He let his jaw drop in mock shock and sucked in an exaggerated breath that had her biting back a smile. "I will have you know that most women would give their left eyeball to be able to sit around and stare at me all day."

"I'm not saying the view isn't impressive."

He gave her a little bow of thanks.

"That doesn't change the fact that I really need to get a few things done."

The thought of her wandering willy-nilly around the city on her own sent a bolt of terror through him so strong he gripped the back of the couch. All he could see in his mind was her lying in a pool of blood somewhere without anyone to help her. Overreaction? Completely. But he was still gluing himself to her side.

"Okay, fine. If you need to go shopping then I will take you."

Her eyes widened. "You're going to take me shopping?"

"Yeah."

"Happily follow me around while I stock up on supplies for my classroom?"

"I didn't say happily, but I have no intention of letting you go by yourself, so you make a list and I'll get my driver and we'll get it done."

"Okay," she said. "But you're going to hate it. Don't say I didn't warn you."

"I consider myself fairly warned."

She smiled at him with a wicked little grin.

"Wait," he said. "What's all that about?" He waved a finger at her smiling face.

"Nothing."

"Exactly how many places are we talking about?"

She shrugged and started wandering around the apartment gathering her things. He followed her like the little lapdog he was turning into. "I don't know. As many as it takes."

"And how many will that be?"

"I don't know."

"Leah?"

"What?"

"Tell me."

"I don't know."

Then she giggled and walked up to the bedroom to get her shoes. Brooks rubbed his hand over his face. This didn't bode well.

# Chapter Twelve

The driver pulled up in front of Brooks's office building and came around to open the door for Leah.

Before she could climb out, Brooks held her back. "You sure you're feeling okay?"

She rolled her eyes. "You need to stop asking me that."

He just stared at her until she sighed. "Yes," she said, giving him the most reassuring smile she could. "The doctor said to take it easy. He didn't say I had to stay comatose."

Brooks didn't look convinced. She climbed out and Brooks jumped out his own side and came around to join her. No sooner had he put his arm around her waist than there was a shout from someone on the sidewalk. They glanced over and flash bulbs started going off.

Brooks gave them a tight smile and tried to hurry her into the building. But more cameras had joined the first and it took Brooks's driver to help clear the path so they could get in the door.

"Are you okay?" he asked her once they were safely inside.

She took a deep breath. "It's not always like that, is it?"

"No, it's usually not this bad. But then I'm not usually escorting my new bride around town."

She held back a groan. "I hope they get sick of me soon."

"Hey," he said, holding the elevator door open for her. "You married one of the most eligible bachelors in town. That's bound to get a little attention now and then."

"Lucky me," she murmured.

Brooks laughed.

Leah's heart rate had barely returned to normal when they reached the top floor. But then the elevator doors opened, and OMG.

She grabbed Brooks's arm. "Brooks. That's…that's…" She pointed at the man who'd graced posters all over her teenaged self's wall.

Brooks glanced down at her with a slight frown. "I know. You okay down there?"

She would have answered, but the man of her girlhood dreams chose that moment to put down the magazine he'd been reading to stand up and greet them.

"Hey, man," Brooks said, holding out his hand. "Sorry I'm a little late. I think we ran into a couple of your buddies outside."

They all laughed and the men did that guy shoulder-bump thing.

"Naw, you can keep them all," he said with a laugh. "Besides, I'm pretty sure they were here for you. I was just a bonus. I didn't have this lovely lady on my arm," he said with a smile at Leah.

Holy crap. One of the world's biggest stars had just called her a lovely lady and was looking at her like he expected some sort of response. She opened her mouth and nothing but a weird squeak came out. Brooks looked at her like she'd suddenly turned a crazy shade of neon purple. Oh God, she probably *had* turned a crazy shade of neon purple. But she couldn't help it. She'd had a poster of that Gatsby movie with him in his tux holding out a champagne glass on her wall in college.

The theme song to *Titanic* started playing in her head, drowning out every other thought.

Her arms may have started rising, mimicking that King-of-the-World scene, because Brooks wrapped his arm around her waist and pulled her tightly to him, keeping one arm pinned against his side.

"This is Leah," he said. "I'm sure she's very happy to meet you."

Leah nodded, her mind nothing but a jumble of nothingness.

*Near…far…wherever you are…*

"Well, the pleasure is all mine."

She squeaked again and Brooks stared at her in open astonishment.

*Pull it together, woman!*

"Hey there, stranger," Kiersten said, coming up to their group, hugging one of *People* magazine's sexiest men on Earth as if they were old friends.

Then she turned to Leah, her eyes growing wide as she looked at her. Apparently, she did look as bad as she felt. Meaning if she didn't sit down fast, her ass and the floor were going to become very well acquainted. Unfortunately, she didn't think she could blame it on the pregnancy this time. Who would have thought she turned into a starstruck idiot the first time she met a movie star?

"We'll leave you gentlemen to your business," Kiersten said, putting an arm around Leah's waist to lead her into Cole's office.

Brooks watched her walk off, his expression part amusement and part bewilderment. She knew the feeling.

She got into Cole's office and collapsed on the couch, sticking her head between her knees.

"I can't believe I made a total ass of myself."

Kiersten laughed. "Are you kidding? You did great. The first time I met him I spilled coffee in his lap."

"You did?" Leah asked, peeking up from behind a curtain of hair.

"Yup. I think these boys forget that we aren't used to palling around with the A-listers of the world. I'm not sure if they just like to see the reaction, or if they honestly don't realize how running into someone like that can affect a newbie."

"How long did it take you to get used to it?"

Kiersten snorted. "I'll let you know when it happens. You should have seen me when I met the *Game of Thrones* cast."

"You met the whole cast?"

Kiersten nodded and Leah squeaked again. "Oh my God. I'd have died."

"You have no idea. We met them on location. They were all in full costume and everything."

"What happened?"

"A couple of them hugged me and I started crying."

Leah laughed. "You didn't."

"Oh yeah, I did. I'm a massive fan. It was a little overwhelming to be standing in a castle being hugged by the friggin King of the North himself."

"What did Cole do?"

She shrugged. "Pretty much what Brooks just did. Stared at me like I had lost my mind. And then left me at home the next time he went to the set." They both laughed and Kiersten shrugged. "I was also pregnant at the time so I'm sure the hormones didn't help either one of us."

"But you were so calm and collected out there in the lobby."

"Only because I've met him a few times. Trust me, there is a whole list of people I'm not allowed to meet because I'd be a puddle of goo on the floor the moment they walked through the door."

"Good to know," Leah said, putting her head back between her knees. "Get celebrities in here often?" She hoped she wouldn't run into any other Hollywood heartthrob on the way out. She'd had her fill for one day.

"It depends on your definition of often. And celebrity."

"Great."

Kiersten laughed. "Hey, you're a celebrity yourself now, you know."

"What are you talking about?"

"That," Kiersten said, pointing at the magazine on the table.

Leah risked sitting up enough to see the tabletop. There were three or four magazines spread on top, each one sporting some version of the headline *Billionaire Takes a Bride*, with a grainy photo of her and Brooks coming out of the courthouse.

"You've got to be kidding," she said, her head rapidly clearing. "It's been less than a week."

Kiersten shrugged. "I'm kind of surprised it took that long."

"Why didn't you warn me there would be pictures of me all over the media?"

She shrugged again. "I thought you knew that going in. Brooks isn't exactly a random country boy. And you saw what happened when I married Cole."

Leah sighed. She fit in with this type of life about as well as a cuddly baby panda would fit in with a pack of hyenas. It had never occurred to her that people would be interested in her or her private life because of who she married. Yes, she knew Brooks was a bit of a celebrity. But she was a nobody. Although thinking of it that way, she could see why everyone assumed it would be a story. One magazine proclaimed it the Cinderella story of the year. Another showed a picture of Brooks with a stunningly beautiful woman on his arm with the grainy photo of her from the wedding up in the corner asking who the mystery woman was as if Leah was the shady "other woman."

"Are you okay?" Brooks asked, popping his head in the door.

Leah stuck her thumb up and kept her head down. Brooks came in and slumped down next to her on the couch.

"Sorry. Should have warned you he might be here. We had a meeting set up, but I thought he cancelled it."

He looked her up and down. "I'd say I was jealous you were fainting all over yourself for another man, but I'm pretty sure I was the same way the first time I met him. I won't even tell you what I did when Gal Gadot walked through the door last month."

Her eyebrows rose and she glanced at Kiersten, who nodded. "Yeah. Wonder Woman applies to her in every sense of the word. I'm half in love with her myself."

"Truth," Brooks said, and Leah elbowed him. He chuckled.

Leah sat up slowly. "What on earth is a megastar actor doing in your office?"

"We're helping him develop an app for one of his green living companies."

"Cool," she said. Lamest answer ever, but she couldn't for the life of her think of anything else to say.

"So, what were you ladies discussing?"

"Leah's new celebrity status," Kiersten said, pointing down to all the magazines.

"Well that didn't take long, did it?" Brooks said, picking one up and looking at the picture.

"What didn't take long?" Cole asked, coming in trailed

by Harrison and Chris.

Brooks pointed down at the magazines.

"Oh yeah. Those." Cole shook his head.

Harrison picked one up and flipped through it. "Heh," he said. "Did you know that only thirty-six percent of those polled think you guys will make it past the six-month mark?"

"What?" Leah asked. "When did we become a poll?"

"One of the late-night shows started a Twitter poll when your wedding picture hit the internet to see how long you guys will last."

"Lovely," Leah said, her head growing fuzzy again.

"Which one?" Brooks asked.

Harrison showed him the article and Brooks grimaced. "Remind me to take him off the Christmas card list."

Leah looked at him, eyes wide. "He's on your Christmas card list?" Then she held up a hand. "Never mind. Of course he is." She dropped her head back between her knees.

Harrison continued. "Looks like twenty-three percent think you won't make it past three months and thirty-nine percent are betting on less than one."

"A whole two percent think we'll make it beyond six months?"

"Well, considering the reputation of the groom..." Harrison said.

Brooks flipped him off.

"Don't blame the messenger," Harrison said.

"They're crazy," Kiersten said. "I think you guys make a wonderful couple."

Leah snorted. "Don't look at me. I'm kind of surprised we made it to the wedding."

Brooks laughed. "Come on, baby. I have total faith it will go the distance."

"I guess it depends on your definition of distance," Chris said.

"Well, hell, anyone want to put their money where their mouth is?" Cole asked.

"Cole. No," Kiersten said, shaking her head.

"Put me down for six months," Harrison said, slapping a hundred-dollar bill on the table.

Kiersten gaped at him. "Don't you start."

Cole's hundred joined it. "You guys forget, I've known him longer than you. I say three months, tops."

Brooks flipped him off too.

Chris slapped his down. "One month." He glanced at Leah. "No offense meant to you at all. It's totally him."

She raised her hand, waving off his concern. "I get it."

"Hey," Brooks said. "Okay, fine." He slapped his own bill on the table. "We make it to end game. Baby day."

Leah and Kiersten glanced at each other, both shaking their heads.

"They'll bet on anything," Leah said.

"Probably my fault," Kiersten said. "I kind of got the whole office pool thing started before Cole and I got together. Now it's a thing. If they can bet on it, they will."

"Lucky me."

Kiersten just grinned at her. "It's not so bad. It's amazing what you can get away with when they are trying to win a bet."

• • •

Leah had never wanted to take a picture of something so badly in her life. Brooks stood in the middle of her classroom, hands out, fingers spread with a piece of tape dangling off of each digit, with streamers of classroom decorations hanging from around his neck and off both arms. He was like a little grade school Christmas tree whose eyes had glazed over.

She went to get another piece of tape from a finger and

stared up at him until he blinked and glanced down.

"Did you go to your happy place?"

His forehead crinkled in a little frown though his lips were twitching into a smile. "My happy place is so far removed from here I can't even find it at the moment."

She grinned up at him. "I told you that you wouldn't have fun."

"Yes, well there's being told something and then experiencing it. My apologies. Next time I promise I'll listen."

"Uh-huh." She stuck another decoration to the wall and then grabbed her stapler, waving him over so he could follow behind her as she tacked up the word chart. She climbed up a small step stool to position the banner, and slapped her palm against the stapler flat against the wall to staple it in.

A buzzing came from her pocket and she fumbled the phone out with one hand.

"Here," she said, "hold this." She thrust the stapler at him. He glanced at her helplessly. With both hands covered in tape there wasn't much he could do. She frowned. He opened his mouth with a sigh.

She placed it carefully inside. "Don't bite down too hard."

He rolled his eyes but kept the stapler firm while she quickly texted Kiersten back. When she turned back around it was to see Brooks staring at her with an expression she wasn't sure she wanted to translate.

"Sorry about that," she said, removing the stapler from his mouth.

He stared at her for a moment, his eyes level with hers for once since she was on the stool. Before she could register his intentions, he had her against the wall, putting his mouth to much better use. Leah mentally protested for half a second before she chucked caution to the wind and joined him in absolute madness. She wrapped one leg around his hip and he growled, grabbing her thigh to anchor his grip. He pressed hard against her while his tongue delved into her mouth and she gasped, tangling her hand in his hair to keep him imprisoned.

"Excuse me!" Mother Genevieve said with a tone caught somewhere between astonishment, disapproval, and perhaps a bit of admiration.

Leah pushed away from Brooks, though he seemed reluctant to let her go.

"I'm so sorry," she said, climbing down from the stool. She brought a hand up to her mouth, quickly wiping her lips and patting at her hair, hoping she wasn't too disheveled.

"I thought I'd stop in and see how things are going," Mother Genevieve said. "Make sure you are all ready for the beginning of the school year."

Leah glanced around her classroom. Everywhere but at Brooks. If she met his gaze right then she'd have probably melted into a puddle of shame right there on the floor. "I think everything is ready to go. Just putting up some visual aids and decorations."

The Reverend Mother also looked around, nodding her head in approval. "Very well. Continue. With your preparations, that is," she said with a pointed look at Brooks who grinned at her. She swept out and Leah sank into the chair behind her desk, covering her face with her hands.

"Oh my gosh, that was so embarrassing."

Brooks shrugged and started removing the tape from his fingers. "Why? We *are* married after all. I thought the whole perk of the old ball and chain deal was the legal right, and even obligation, to grope my wife anytime and anywhere."

Leah opened her mouth to respond and then closed it again.

"Ha. See. I actually have a valid point for once."

She gave him a slow smile. "You do."

"Who texted you?"

"Huh? Oh," she said, trying to get her brain to focus on something other than the hard body she'd just been wrapped around. "Um, it was Kiersten. She wants to know if I can watch Piper next week while she and Cole go to dinner. Their nanny is out of town for a few weeks. I told her that would be fine."

"What day?"

"Next Friday."

He thought for a moment and then nodded. "That should be fine. I don't have anything going on that night."

Leah blinked at him, trying to process what he'd said. "You want to babysit with me? As in watching an actual baby. Taking care of one, I mean."

"I'm not letting you go by yourself. You're supposed to be taking it easy. In fact, it would probably be best if they brought the baby to my place."

Leah took a deep breath. "Brooks, while I am flattered and think it is beyond sweet that you are so concerned for me you really have got to stop this. I am totally fine. The doctor has cleared me. I am capable of going uptown and watching a baby for a few hours without you glued to my side."

"I know you're capable…"

But she shook her head. "I know you're concerned and I know it was a scary night, but it's over with. I'm fine now. And frankly you're driving me freaking insane. You can't keep me locked up in your apartment forever."

His concern melted away into a playfully naughty look. "Well now there's an idea I could get behind."

He took her hand and pulled her out of the chair, intertwining her fingers with his and pinning them behind her back to press her closer. "I can keep you locked up in my bedroom…" He kissed her. "Maybe even tie you up." He kissed her again with a quick nip at her lip that sent a jolt of fire straight to her core. "Keep you my prisoner and have my way with you until you're screaming my name."

She sucked in a tremulous breath and he leaned down and captured her lips again. He let go of her hands so Leah could drag her arms around his neck and hold on for dear mercy. When he finally let her go, her head swam in a sea of hormones that drowned out any lingering concern. Who cared if he followed her around like some crazed overzealous bodyguard? As long as he took a break every now and then to do that again.

"Maybe it's not so much concern," he said, resting his forehead against hers. "Maybe I just want to be with you."

She cleared her throat, trying to regain her composure. "Oh?"

"Yeah."

"You find me that entertaining, do you?"

"Hell yeah," he said with that mischievously crooked grin that sent her insides quivering.

"Well, don't plan on being too entertained. That might get us into trouble. The doctor hasn't cleared me for everything yet."

Brooks released an exaggerated, long-suffering sigh that brought a smile to her lips.

"Good point. Still, it would be easier on you if they brought the baby to us."

She patted his cheek. "If that makes you feel better, I'll tell her." She took a second to shoot off another text to Kiersten and then gathered up her things. She slung her bag over her shoulder, leaving several bags for him to carry. "But if you're going to be there, you have to actually help."

He draped two bags over each shoulder. "I don't think I mentioned anything about helping."

"Hey, you're the one insisting being there. You're not just going to sit and watch me do all the work."

"Well, yeah, but…"

"Actually, this might be a great idea," Leah said, enjoying watching him squirm. "Babies are a lot of work, and you're the one who wants me to take it easy, so maybe *you* could take care of her and I'll watch *you*."

"Wait," he said, hot on her heels.

"Oh, no worries. You'll do fine. Babies are easy. You just have to make sure she's fed, changed, and burped, and that she gets her naps, is kept clean, and that she doesn't roll off or under anything. She's not crawling yet so that's not a problem. Of course, babies poop a lot, but I'm sure you'll handle that fine."

"Wait, did you say poop?" He hurried after her, but every time he got in her path she moved around him, trying and failing to keep the smile from her face.

"Leah, I heard poop. There's going to be poop? I think I've changed my mind."

Her phone dinged and she looked down at the message, her grin widening. "Sorry, too late. I already told her to bring the baby over and that you're helping out. She loves the idea. Thinks it'll be good for you. Said you used to work wonders with barnyard animals. You're going to have to tell me about that sometime."

He scowled. "There was an incident with a cow that I've vowed never to speak of again."

Leah stopped in her tracks and Brooks bumped into her, doing a little hopping dance to keep from running over her without dropping all the bags.

"A cow?" she asked. "Kiersten needs to spill the beans on that one if you won't."

She started walking again, leaving Brooks still fumbling with the bags. He caught up quickly enough. "I think I just remembered I have to do something that night."

"Not a problem, you can cancel it."

She marched off to the car, laughing while Brooks

scurried behind her, coming up with one excuse after another. There was no way she was letting him off the hook after he insisted on being there.

Oh, this was going to be fun.

Leah pushed aside the stack of essays she was supposed to be grading and went back to staring at the screen with the cursor blinking at her. She had no idea what else she could say. She'd been sending regular messages to Marcus, using the Facebook messages almost as a pregnancy journal. She hadn't wanted to tell him over the computer like that, but since she couldn't get ahold of him and her belly wasn't getting any smaller, she didn't want to blindside him after the baby was born.

So she finally broke the news and then had begun keeping him updated. Every time she went to an appointment she'd send a message saying how it went. She'd uploaded photos of the sonograms, even a clip of the baby's heartbeat that Brooks had recorded. She had gone back and forth on whether she should tell Marcus about Brooks. It seemed wrong not to, so she'd finally mentioned that she was married now. Of course, she hadn't gone much further than that and she certainly hadn't told him the real circumstances of their marriage. She did tell him Brooks's name, though. He had a right to know who the stepfather of his child was, even if the marriage wouldn't last much longer.

Mostly, she just stuck to the baby. But she couldn't go on sending him Facebook messages forever. She'd stop once the baby was born. He could get ahold of her if he wanted to after that.

She sent the message off and sat back, her hands cradling her belly.

"Still no response?" Brooks came up behind her and rested his hands on her shoulders.

She sat back and shook her head. "No, but I don't know what else I can try."

He leaned in closer, looking at the image on the screen. His hands tightened on her shoulders. "Wait…is that the father? Marcus Cassidy?"

"Yes. Do you know him?" she asked.

When he didn't answer right away she glanced up to see him glaring at Marcus's profile picture, his jaw clenched. She shifted under the pressure of his fingers and he snapped out of it, easing his grip.

"Sorry. Yes, I know him. Knew him. A long time ago. We went to college together."

"And?"

He shrugged. "It was several years ago."

"It doesn't seem like knowing him was a good thing."

He gave her a half smile. "When you have two roosters in a hen house a few feathers are going to fly."

She laughed. "Where did you hear an expression like that?"

His grin was more genuine this time. "I picked up a couple good ones on the last poker retreat Kiersten planned for us. Which is why she's no longer allowed to plan our retreats, by the way."

"I really need to get some details from her one of these days."

Brooks ignored that and went back to semi-glaring at the computer. "Have you considered the possibility that he's read the messages but has chosen not to respond?"

"Yes." That didn't really answer her question, though maybe it did. Brooks didn't seem to think much of Marcus. And though the thought probably should hurt, it didn't. It might even be a relief if he didn't want anything to do with the baby. It would at least make things less complicated.

She sighed. "But there's no icon. See," she said, pointing to the screen. "A little check mark appears when the message has been delivered and when the person has read the message their profile picture appears in a little bubble next to it. So as far as I can tell he hasn't seen these yet. But I don't have any other way to communicate with him. His whole account is set to private. It won't allow anyone to post on the wall, only send messages. I can't even see his friends list to try and contact him through them."

"Do you want me to try and find him?" Brooks asked quietly.

"Will you?" She turned to look at him but couldn't read what he might be thinking. His face was a total blank. "You would do that?"

"If you asked me to."

She hesitated. She didn't want to hurt Brooks and she had a feeling if she said she wanted his help in finding Marcus that it would hurt him. But at the same time, Brooks wasn't always going to be there and Marcus *was* the baby's father. He did have every right to know. Once he knew, they could deal with it then. But Leah wanted to make sure she did what she could to let him know that he had a child.

"If you think you might be able to help, that would be great," she said.

Brooks nodded and looked at the screen. "Is this all the information you have on him?"

"Yeah," she said, trying to stamp down the familiar rush of embarrassment that she'd had a one-night stand with a man she'd never met and had no intention of seeing again.

There was no judgment on Brooks's face. "I'll see what I can do."

"Thank you."

He gave her a small smile and kissed her on the forehead

and then left the room.

Leah sighed and put her hands on her belly. "I don't know what to do, little peanut," she said. "The father you have doesn't know you exist and the father I want you to have..."

She stopped, not realizing until the moment she said it out loud how true the words were. She glanced back at the door through which Brooks had disappeared. "The father I want you to have is probably better off without us," she whispered.

Brooks had seemed happy over the last few months, but there was no denying she was cramping his lifestyle. She still felt more like a guest in his apartment than someone in her own home. Despite a few feminine touches here and there, the place was most definitely a bachelor pad. The furniture was stark and cold, all steel and leather and glass; not an environment you wanted a baby learning how to walk in. And while people raised babies in the city every day, Leah had always envisioned raising her child in a less hectic environment.

At the school, at least, they were on the outskirts and behind the stone walls with all its gardens and quiet corridors. The world would have been a bit smaller. Ideally, she wanted the whole white picket fence thing. It was a clichéd dream, but she couldn't help envisioning her little one running around on the back lawn, maybe playing on a swing set, learning to ride a bike on a quiet cul-de-sac, playing with friends in the summer. Leah was fairly sure she'd be a nervous wreck raising her baby on the busy streets of New York City. She would do what she needed to, of course. Even though she wouldn't stay there forever, she knew she was more fortunate than most of the world's population. So while it wasn't exactly what she dreamed of, she would be grateful for every moment she spent there. With him.

And when it was over...well, she wouldn't think of that just yet.

# Chapter Thirteen

"So how's it going?" Cole asked.

He and Brooks sat on the couch while the women were on the floor on the other side of the living room watching as the baby lay on her back kicking her feet in the air.

"All right," Brooks said.

Cole raised his eyebrows and waited.

Brooks didn't say anything for a second. "I told Leah I'd help her get ahold of the father."

"So why do you sound so pissed about it?"

"The father is Marcus Cassidy."

Cole's eyes widened. "Douchebag Cassidy from college?"

Brooks nodded and Cole gave a low whistle. "Well, shit."

"Yeah."

"Does she know about him?"

"What, that the guy is a total dick who made it his mission in life to screw me over? No."

"Well, maybe she should."

Brooks waved that off. "It'll look like I'm jealous of the asshat."

"So are you still going to try and find him?"

"I already did. I left a message through his secretary that he needed to check his Facebook messages."

Cole raised a brow. "That's pretty vague."

Brooks shrugged. "Maybe, but I said I'd try and find the guy, not that I'd bring him to her wrapped in a neat little bow."

"You think he'll respond?"

"My gut reaction is no. Under normal circumstances. But…she told him that she's married to me."

Cole sat back. "If he reads those messages he'll know that the woman carrying his child is married to you."

"Yeah."

"Holy shit."

Brooks sighed. "Yeah."

"You need to warn her about him."

"Anything I say is going to come off wrong. What am I supposed to do? Tell her that if the guy does come around, it's only because he's got some weird complex about always besting me and stealing my wife would be the epitome of that?"

"Something like that."

"I can't do that. Hopefully, he'll see the word baby and run screaming in the other direction."

"Yeah, hopefully." Though Cole didn't look even slightly convinced that would happen. "So, other than baby daddy drama, how are things? You know…with the whole marriage thing?"

"Fine."

"Just fine?"

"Put the meddling mother tone away," Brooks said. "It can't be going much more than fine until the doctor says everything's good to go. And even then I'd be terrified to touch her."

"Man," Cole said, slapping him on the knee, "don't worry

about it. It happens. It's really common."

"Really? Did it happen when Kiersten was pregnant?"

"Well no, but it's in all the baby books. The doctor said everything is good, right?"

"Yeah. I don't know, though, and to be honest it's something I've been trying hard not to think about."

"I can understand that. In the meantime, are you sure you're up to this?" Cole nodded his head at his offspring.

"Sure. I mean, how hard can it be?"

Cole looked at him and laughed.

"Way to be ominous, bro."

That only made Cole laugh harder.

Kiersten and Leah came over to join them, Kiersten jostling the baby on her hip. "What's so funny over here?"

Cole stood up and kissed her on the cheek. "Brooks said he thinks this will be a piece of cake."

Kiersten looked over at him and grinned. "Just like the cow would be a piece of cake."

"Hey. Vow," Brooks said.

Leah looked back and forth between them all. "Okay, I'm definitely being left out of an inside joke here."

Brooks sighed. "It peed on me. And that's all I'm saying about it."

Leah's jaw dropped and Brooks shook his head, not wanting to relive the memory.

"And on that note," Kiersten said, "we've got to get going."

She handed him the baby, startling Brooks too much to do anything but take her, though he had assumed Leah would be doing most of the baby work. He held the baby under her arms, letting her legs dangle in the air, but he didn't know how long he could keep that up. She squirmed much more than he'd anticipated.

"She's not a bomb, Brooks," Kiersten said. "Hold her

back against your body."

He'd seen it done in movies and in the park, but he hadn't had any younger siblings to practice on, and he hadn't been around babies much. He did what Kiersten said, tucking his arms under the baby's legs and holding her back against his chest. It still didn't feel comfortable but he did have a better grip on her.

"Okay, we'll be back in a few hours," Kiersten said. "Have fun, you two."

She glanced at Leah and they shared a look. Leah grinned and walked them to the elevator. Piper started squirming again and arching back against him. He didn't want to put her on the floor so he sat her up on the couch, but she promptly slid to her side. She didn't seem uncomfortable, though, so he left her lying there while he went to get her blanket. He spun around when he heard Leah gasp.

"What? What is it? What's wrong?"

She took two giant steps toward the couch, arms out, catching the baby before she rolled off.

"You can't leave babies unattended like that," she said.

"But she wasn't unattended. I was right here. I turned around for a second."

"That's all it takes."

"I didn't know she could roll like that. I thought she'd stay put."

Leah laughed. "Babies never stay put. You can't leave them someplace where they might roll off. Either build a barrier with pillows or strap her in her bouncy chair or something. Or just lay her on the floor. She'll be fine."

Brooks took a deep breath trying to keep his heart from pounding straight out of his chest. He'd been in charge for less than a minute and he'd already almost killed the baby. Her parents probably weren't even out of the elevator yet.

"I think this was a bad idea," he said.

Leah laughed again. "Don't worry. You'll be fine." She handed Piper back to him. "I have to use the restroom. Will you be okay on your own for a minute?"

Brooks looked at the squirming bundle smiling up at him. "Sure, but…hurry back, okay?"

She grinned at him and shook her head. "Don't leave her alone on any high surfaces."

"No high surfaces. Got it."

He sat on the couch, but Piper kept wriggling in his arms. "Are you bored? Do you want to lie down? What do you want?"

She blinked up at him with her big blue eyes and shoved her little fist in her mouth. A line of drool leaked from between her chubby fingers as she chewed on it…heading straight for his shirt. He glanced around trying to find something to catch the mess. Her diaper bag sat a few feet away at the end of the couch. He went to put her down and then remembered rule number one: no leaving the baby alone on high surfaces. So he carried her with him, taking care to keep her face away from his shirt.

He rummaged through the diaper bag unearthing diapers, wipes, assorted bottles of powders and ointments, toys, bottles, formula mix, extra outfits, changing pads… there had to be something in there to catch the… Oh there it was!

He grabbed a square of cloth and wiped the baby's chin and fist, but his shirt was already a goner, smeared with baby drool. He sighed and smiled down at her.

"Looks like your daddy's footing the dry-cleaning bill this month," he said. Piper grinned back up at him. Cute little thing, he had to admit that.

He held her up a little higher. "You know, I've always wondered why people get so goofy over babies." He held her out so she could see his face. She giggled and swatted at him.

He laughed. "You guys are kind of cute, though, aren't you? Aren't you?" he said again, his voice changing an octave. "Yes, you are. I don't know why I'm talking like this. But I can't seem to stop. It's contagious, I think. Baby-itis. Are you contaminated? I think you are. I'm going to talk like this forever, aren't I? Yes, I am. You're just adorable. Definitely take after your mummy. Not smelly Daddy. No, we don't like him."

He held her over his head, jostling her around to make her laugh. She giggled harder so he continued to do it, even when he heard the bathroom door open. Sure, there was a slight sense of embarrassment, but that was overshadowed by the adorable sounds coming out of the little creature in his hands.

"Brooks, you might want to be careful," Leah said.

"Careful of what? She's just adorable. Couldn't hurt a fly. No, she couldn't," he said in that annoying baby voice that people get around anything younger than a teenager, that he seriously couldn't stop doing.

"Aren't you? You're a tiny little thing. What could you possibly do—"

There was no warning, no sign of distress. No scrunched-up face. No cry. The baby went from an adorable giggling machine to an *Exorcist*-worthy vomit fountain in under a second. It happened so fast he didn't even know how to react, just stood there blinking the warm liquid from his eyes as Piper began to fuss.

Oh, sure. *Now* she cries.

Leah hurried over and took her from him, handing him a towel.

"Would now be a bad time to say I told you so?" she asked, blinking at him with her best angelic face.

"Yep," he said. "Going to have to take a rain check on that, if it's all the same to you."

"Gotcha. I'll pencil that in for later. Though, to avoid a repeat, it's good to be a little careful when the baby has just eaten. Kiersten fed her right before they left."

"Ah," he said, dabbing at his face. "Good to know. Though really…how does something so tiny produce such a large volume of something so disgusting?"

Leah laughed and the baby followed along with her.

"Oh sure," he said. "I bet you two are getting a kick out of this, aren't you?" he said, the baby voice popping out again.

Leah pulled out her phone and took a quick snapshot. Brooks held out his hands to block his face, but it was too late.

"Oh, this is so going to be my new profile picture," she said.

"Don't you dare. I'm more than happy to share it with you." He took a threatening step toward her and she flung out a hand to keep him away.

"No, no, okay, you win!" She nodded him in the direction of the bathroom. "Go get cleaned up. I'll take care of the baby."

"Okay. Just be careful of that," he said, pointing at the baby's little mouth, "and that." He pointed to the diaper region. "I've heard things can get pretty bad down there too."

Leah laughed again and shooed him away. "Don't worry, I can handle it."

He walked out, glancing back once to watch her as she cradled the baby. The scene was so domestic, something he had never expected to see in his living room. Not in his lifetime. But somehow it felt incredibly right. Surreal beyond a doubt. But right. For the first time, a profound sense of regret filled him that the happy little scene couldn't last. A small part of him whispered *why can't it?* He shook his head and pushed that back into the deep, dark box from which it had crawled. He and Leah hadn't known each other very long, not long enough for him to screw it up, but he had no doubt he would remedy that soon enough.

He always did.

• • •

Leah finished burping the baby and looked over at Brooks who sat in an armchair scrolling through his tablet. It was crazy how normal it all felt, how much like a family they seemed. For a few hours, she'd forgotten that everything was fake and had even allowed herself to imagine that they were home with their own baby. She needed to nip that kind of thinking in the bud. It would only make things harder down the road.

"Can you take Piper for a minute?" she asked, bringing her over. "I need to get dinner started."

He blinked up at her in surprise. "We could order something."

She smiled. He couldn't fool her. His desire for takeout had more to do with his fear of being left alone with the baby again than it did with any culinary preferences.

"Hold her for a minute. She's almost asleep."

Brooks reluctantly held out his arms and she laid the sleepy baby in them, leaning down to give Piper's head a kiss.

"There, see," she said. "She likes you." Brooks glanced down at the baby uncertainly, but nodded at Leah when she gave him a questioning look.

"Don't go too far."

"I'll be in the kitchen right behind you."

She busied herself in the kitchen getting things ready, quickly chopping vegetables and dicing chicken for a stir-fry. Every now and then she glanced up to make sure Brooks hadn't exploded in a shower of baby-induced panic. He seemed to be handling things okay.

She got everything ready and dished out, and turned to

call him to the table, but the sight that met her stopped her in her tracks. Quiet fussing noises came from the baby. Brooks had her tucked against his chest while he gently rocked her and the faint sound of his singing floated to her. The sight of him singing about sunshine and rainbows, the tiny bundle cradled in his muscular arms, sent a wave of emotion through Leah so strong she had to grip the chair. She didn't even know how to process the chaos tumbling around inside her. It was beyond adorable, incredibly sweet, and if she wasn't already pregnant this probably would have knocked her up on the spot.

What was it about a big strong man cradling a tiny baby that was so damn sexy?

He glanced up at her and saw her watching him, but instead of getting embarrassed like she thought he would, he smiled. Not his usual over-the-top goofy grin, but a tender, happy smile that, at once, looked so out of place and yet right at home on his face.

"Dinner's ready," she said to him, speaking quietly so as not to disturb the newly settled baby.

He glanced down. "What do I do with her?"

Leah waved him over to where she'd set up a playpen.

"Set her down in there so she can nap while we eat."

He gently deposited the precious bundle into the playpen and then stood at the side, gazing down. "They're really cute when they're sleeping, aren't they?"

She laughed quietly. "Pretty cute when they're awake, too."

Brooks nodded. "Well, except for when she's doing her *Exorcist* imitation. But other than that, yeah, sure."

They laughed again and she took his hand to draw him into the kitchen. "Sit. Eat."

He picked up a fork and stared down at the food.

"What's the matter?" she asked, putting a napkin in her

lap. "You don't like stir-fry?"

"No, I love it. It's not that. It's…I don't think I've had an actual home-cooked meal since the last time my mom came to visit."

"Don't you cook?"

He snorted. "I've attempted it a few times. It didn't go well."

"Oh, come on. I'm sure it wasn't that bad."

"Freshman year of college. I wanted to impress this girl I liked. So I invited her to my dorm room for a home-cooked meal."

"To your dorm room?"

He nodded. "I had one of those hot plate things. And a microwave. I figured I was set."

"And?"

"Well, I had her in bed by nine."

Leah raised her eyebrows, waiting for the punch line.

"Except it wasn't the bed I'd covered in black silk sheets, it was a bed in the ER and she was puking her guts out with food poisoning. The ER doc said it was the worst case he'd ever seen."

He shook his head, his eyes focused on the long-ago past. "I'd never felt so bad about anything in my life. I'd tried really hard, too. Found some fancy recipe in one of those Martha Stewart magazines. Blew a whole paycheck and an entire day sweating over that stupid little hot plate. I don't think it got quite hot enough, though."

"I'm sure she appreciated the effort."

He laughed, though there was no amusement in the sound. "Naw, she'd wanted me to take her to some fancy restaurant that had just opened because that's where her roommate's boyfriend had taken her. But that guy had a rich daddy and a big allowance. I had a hard-working dad who was barely making ends meet himself and a job delivering pizzas at night to help pay for college. So I borrowed some of those little white Christmas lights from a friend in the Theater Club and strung them all over my room, cleaned it up real nice. You know, tried to make it all romantic."

"It sounds wonderful," Leah said, her heart aching for him. He told the story with a smile, but his eyes held a lingering pain that she wished she could erase.

"You'd have thought I'd taken her to some back alley and tried to feed her dumpster drippings. She choked down a couple bites and finally spit it out and asked what kind of a cheapskate moron would try to cook an edible meal in a dorm room."

"That's horrible!"

He shrugged. "She wasn't wrong. I mean, she did end up in the ER."

Leah's heart cracked a little more. She had half a mind to find out who that girl was so she could go defend his honor or something. What a despicable way to treat someone.

"She was wrong. Whether it met her expectations or not, you went to a lot of trouble and she was nothing but a…a… bitch."

That startled a genuine laugh out of him. "I didn't know you had such a potty mouth, Little Miss Schoolteacher."

"I only use it on special occasions."

"Good to know you have a naughty side," he said with a wink.

Oh, she had a very naughty side. But letting it out to play would be incredibly ill-advised so she ignored that remark. "If it's any consolation, I know how you must have felt."

"You've given someone food poisoning, too?"

She laughed. "No. But I've gone to extreme effort only to have it thrown back in my face. A guy I'd been dating for over a year ended up moving so we tried the long-distance thing for a while. He had to fly into a city that was about an hour or so from me for a business meeting. We were supposed to meet up when he was done, but I knew the meeting wasn't going well and I wanted to surprise him. I went and bought all his favorite candies, wrote out a bunch of notes about the things I loved about him, and placed them all around his hotel room so he'd find them when he got out of his meeting."

"And he didn't like it?"

She frowned at the unwelcome memory. "I didn't hear from him for two days. I'd been supposed to meet him at the hotel. It's why I had the key for his room. But since he didn't call me to tell me when he got back, I assumed…well, I didn't know what to think. He wouldn't return any of my messages. He finally answered the phone two days later. Didn't mention his hotel room at all so when I brought it up, he said he thought it was kind of stalkery and it had made him uncomfortable so he'd left and gone back home."

"He thought it was stalkery for a woman he'd been dating for a year to go into a hotel room to which she'd been invited to spread around some love notes and candy to cheer him up when he'd had a bad day?"

"Yeah."

Brooks shook his head. "I think some people are determined to be miserable. You can shower me with love notes and candy anytime you want."

She laughed. "I'll keep that in mind. Now eat before it gets cold. I hope you like it," she said, squirming at the sudden shyness that flooded her.

"I'm sure it'll be amazing."

He gave her a smile that warmed her down to her very core, and she turned her attention to her dinner to break the connection. He was certainly turning out to be more than she'd expected, which was going to be a problem when it came time to say good-bye.

She pushed that thought away. For the moment, she

would enjoy the time they had.

By the time Kiersten and Cole came to pick up Piper, Brooks had exhausted himself in a tornado of baby care. Leah met them at the door with her finger to her lips and gestured them over to the couch where she pointed down at the cutest sight ever. Kiersten put her hand over her mouth and smiled and then whipped out her phone. Cole shook his head while his wife snapped several pictures, but even he was smiling.

Brooks had fallen asleep on the couch with the baby tucked in one arm, a burp cloth over his shoulder, three teddy bears tucked in around them, and a bottle in his hand. And one of those horseshoe-shaped baby pillows on his head that he had been wearing as a crown to try and get the baby to laugh.

"So it went well then?" Kiersten asked.

"Surprisingly well. I mean, there is obviously a bit of a learning curve," she said, gesturing to the destroyed apartment. "But he started to get the hang of everything. He might not have all the mechanics down of changing diapers and stuff, but he has a way with babies that is pretty cute. He had her smiling and gurgling at him the whole time."

Kiersten beamed. "I'm glad it wasn't too horrible for you guys."

Leah shook her head. "We had fun."

Cole had finished gathering up their things so Kiersten went to collect the baby from Brooks. He startled awake when she took the baby, but quickly settled back down to sleep when he saw that it was her.

Leah walked them to the door and said her good-byes. Then she went back over to the couch and stared down at Brooks for a few moments. He wasn't remotely what she'd expected. In any given situation, he always found some way to surprise her.

Life with him, while it lasted, would never be boring, that was for sure.

The door buzzer sounded and Brooks jumped. Leah laughed. "It's just the door."

"Oh," he said, rubbing his hand over his face.

"I'll see who it is." Leah turned to check the intercom but Brooks stood and stretched.

"It's probably Cole," he said, holding up the baby blanket he'd been snuggling with. "Can't put the princess to bed without her favorite blanket, which I apparently stole from her. You sit. I'll check the door."

He'd popped off the couch and was already at the door checking the video monitor before Leah could respond. She shrugged. She sank onto the couch and leaned her head against the back, glad to get her increasing weight off her feet. Her little peanut was starting to kill her back and feet. She rubbed her hands over her belly, over and over. Feeling the hard mound beneath her fingertips, its wiggling inhabitant safe and snug, had become a soothing gesture for her.

The door buzzer sounded again and Brooks cursed under his breath but buzzed in whoever it was and came back over to her. She glanced at him and at the sight of his face, immediately sat up, her heart thudding in concern.

"Brooks? What's the matter? Who is it?"

He gave her a tight smile. "You have a visitor."

# Chapter Fourteen

Brooks waited by the door, his entire demeanor rigid. Leah's heart dropped. She'd never seen him like that. Ever. Brooks always had a smile in his eyes, no matter what was happening.

"Brooks? What's going on? Who is it?" she asked, but a knock at the door sounded before he could stay a word. Instead of answering her, he just opened it.

She stood, her hands immediately going to her belly as she stared at the man in the doorway. "Marcus," she said, her mind a total blank for a moment as she stared at her baby's father.

Brooks nodded at him as Marcus entered carrying an enormous bouquet of flowers and then glanced at Leah, his expression unreadable. "I'll leave you two alone," he said.

He went into his wine room and turned to close the door, glancing back at her just once.

"Brooks," she said. But he turned away and shut the door. The look on his face nearly tore her heart out.

Marcus walked slowly into the room, his eyes darting between hers and her belly.

"I'm sorry to drop in unannounced, especially so late. But I just got your messages and wanted to see you."

"No, that's fine, really. That's why I gave you the address. In case you ever wanted to…look us up…"

"So, you're really…" His gaze dropped back to the baby bump.

Her brows lifted a little. Had he thought she was lying? "Yes. You say you just saw my messages?"

He smiled a bit sheepishly. "Yeah, I'm sorry I never responded. I've been out of the country for several months and checking Facebook wasn't high on the priority list. Oh, these are for you," he said, handing her the flowers.

"Thank you. They're gorgeous." She went into the kitchen area and laid them on the counter, using the time to try and calm her nerves. What the hell did you say to the guy who knocked you up and then reappeared out of the blue five months later?

"I imagine it was somewhat of a shock to see all that. I'm sorry I broke the news that way, but I didn't know how else to contact you. I thought you should know…"

"No, that's fine. Thank you for trying to get ahold of me. But I'm here now."

"Yes, you are." And what in the hell did that mean? What did she want it to mean? She didn't know this man. He was a total stranger to her, one she'd never meant to see again. And now here they were, bound through the tiny life they'd created.

Someone really needed to write a how-to book that dealt with the subject. *How to Deal with Your One-Night Stand Turned Baby Daddy.* With a bonus chapter on how to juggle a new husband into the mix.

She gestured for him to have a seat on the couch. She sat beside him though she left plenty of room between them.

He glanced around. "You have a great place here."

"Thanks, though I can't take credit. It's Brooks's place."

"But aren't you two married?"

*Oops. Can't forget about that.* "Yes, but Brooks lived here before we got married. I guess I'm still getting used to calling it home."

"Ah, I see."

She nodded and they sat in awkward silence for a minute or two before he nodded at her belly.

"So…is everything going okay with…?"

"Yes," she said, happy to have something to talk about. "Almost twenty weeks now. Baby is growing perfectly. We haven't found out the sex yet…oh. I guess now that you're here I should discuss all that with you. If you want to know or not?"

He waved that off. "Whatever you decide is fine. I'm not going to start making demands about anything the second I walk through the door. I'm just glad to hear everything is going well."

That was nice of him. The nervous butterflies in her gut hadn't eased yet and, finally, she laughed. He raised an eyebrow.

"I'm sorry. It's…this whole situation is a little…"

"Awkward?" he asked with a smile.

"Yes."

He sat forward and took her hands in his. "Look, there's no expectations here. I'd like to be involved as much as possible, but that's entirely up to you. And I know we don't really know each other, but we got along well enough the last time we met." His gaze turned suggestive and his thumbs drew lazy circles over the backs of her hands. "I'm sure we'll get used to each other again in no time."

Her mind went blank for a second. They *had* had a really great time that night. The best she'd ever had until…

She glanced up at the door of the wine room and saw Brooks standing there. "Brooks," she said, pulling her hands out of Marcus's and standing up. She tried to ignore the guilt crashing over her. After all, she'd done nothing wrong. Even if their marriage had been a true one, she'd done nothing. But she still couldn't help the urge to fidget and squirm under Brooks's gaze.

He smiled, though the expression didn't reach his eyes, and came to her, wrapping his arm around her waist, much to her surprise. The gesture calmed her, though, and she leaned against him.

"So, how are things going out here?" he asked, his eyes focused on Marcus.

"Great," Marcus said. "Just getting reacquainted with the mother of my baby."

Leah glanced at him with a slight frown. That had sounded awfully possessive. And the weird tension between the two men was growing by the second.

Brooks's arm tightened around her. "I don't remember if I mentioned that Marcus and I went to school together."

"Yes—" Leah started but Marcus answered first.

"Yes, we did. We were quite the rivals back then, weren't we?" he said, his tone friendly, though there was a look in his eye that bugged Leah.

"Were you?" she asked, glancing up at Brooks. He hadn't taken his gaze from Marcus, but the line of his jaw looked as though he was gritting his teeth.

"Oh, yeah," Marcus said. "Had a couple competing projects. This big guy even lost a few girls to me, I think." He laughed, but Brooks's arm around her tensed.

"Ancient history," Brooks said, with a smile she could tell was forced, though to Marcus it probably looked normal.

"Of course, of course." He looked back at Leah. "I was only at school a couple years before I sold my first app and then I left for bigger and better things."

Brooks didn't answer, and before Marcus could

say anything more, his phone beeped. He glanced at it. "Unfortunately, I need to run. But," he pulled a business card out of his pocket and handed it to Leah, "this has all my contact info on it, and I've written my personal cell phone number on the back. Let me know when your next appointment is and any baby related stuff that goes on. I want to be there for all of it."

"I will," Leah said, genuinely pleased he wanted to be so involved. The brooding presence of Brooks behind her certainly made everything a little more awkward, but having an involved father in the picture would only be good for the baby.

"And please call me if there is anything at all you need," he said. "Even a late-night run for ice cream."

"I think I can manage any ice-cream cravings," Brooks said.

"Of course. But no need to run yourself ragged. There are two of us in the picture now." Marcus laughed and then leaned in to kiss Leah on the cheek. "I'll talk to you soon." He pointed at Brooks. "Take care of our girl." He gave him a big, cheesy grin and waved on his way out.

Leah risked a glance at Brooks who still stood staring at the door.

"I take it the two of you weren't friends back in the day?"

Brooks glanced down at her and snorted. "We were, sort of. Until he sold the app we were working on out from under me."

She opened her mouth to ask more questions, but he said, "It was almost a decade ago," and then headed for the stairs. "It's late. I'm going to turn in." He took the stairs two at a time, leaving her standing in the middle of the loft.

"Well, that was interesting," she muttered.

It had never occurred to her that Brooks and Marcus would have issues getting along. It had never occurred to her they'd ever be in the same room, especially with Marcus taking so long to respond. And even more especially because the odds of her baby daddy and temporary husband knowing each other were beyond slim. Or so she'd thought.

Either way, stressing her out wasn't healthy for the baby and the baby was the only one who mattered here, so the boys were just going to have to kiss and make up. At least until the baby was born and the whole fake marriage thing was over and done with. Then she could figure out where Marcus would fit in with things. And where Brooks fit. If he wanted to fit, which seemed less and less likely.

She took a deep breath. No point in worrying about it now. They had a few months to get all the kinks worked out. Until then, her concern was getting her little peanut safely into a conflict-free world.

• • •

Brooks picked up two cards, biting back a smile at the full house staring back at him. But he must not have done it quick enough.

"Oh, better watch it," Cole said, picking up his own cards. "Looks like Brooks has a good hand over there."

"No, I don't think that's it," Harrison said, his soft British accent making him sound like Sherlock Holmes trying to solve a mystery. "I think something else is going on with him. What could it be?"

He stroked his chin like he was trying to puzzle it out and Brooks flipped him off as he tossed a few more chips into the pile. Harrison chuckled.

Chris looked back and forth between them. "What is it?"

"It's nothing," Brooks said.

Harrison shrugged. "Says you. But your opinion is a little biased, now, isn't it?"

Brooks glared at him, but that only made Harrison smile

wider.

"What?" he finally asked.

Harrison shrugged. "Sorry, mate. Just never thought I'd see this side of you, that's all."

"And what side would that be?" He picked up his beer to chug it down.

"The whole domesticated-bliss-happy-monogamous thing. Don't get me wrong. It suits you. Just not something I ever expected, that's all."

"I don't know what you're talking about," Brooks said.

Except that was a lie. He knew exactly what Harrison meant. Leah had been living with him for two months now and she had completely changed his world. Turned it upside down in a tornado of domesticity that would put Martha Stewart to shame. There was floral-scented shampoo in the shower, makeup everywhere, soft pillows on every available sitting or sleeping surface, candles on every other available flat surface, even curtains on his windows for fuck's sake.

And don't even get him started on the books. The woman had stacks of them everywhere. She'd filled the two bookshelves in his apartment and still he swore every time she came home she had another stack. She was a total neat freak so it's not like they were all over the apartment. But she had begun to stack them up against his walls so it looked as if one whole room was wallpapered in a book motif. How she found the time to read any of them, he didn't know.

Somehow she managed to work a full day at the school, come home and cook dinner, and she couldn't seem to stop straightening up around the house. According to one of the books she'd left lying around, she was nesting, though instead of it being an end of the pregnancy thing, she was going full tilt all the way through. He wouldn't be surprised if his poor housekeeper quit out of sheer boredom.

He would never admit it to his friends, but he *was* happy,

despite all of that. He hadn't had a date with another woman, let alone anything else, since the moment she walked into his life, and he didn't miss it. Oh, he had a massive list of things he wanted to do with her the moment the doctor cleared them, but other women hadn't even crossed his mind.

"See. There it is again," Harrison said.

Brooks looked back up at him.

"What?"

Cole chuckled. "You're grinning like a…how did you put it when you first met her? A twitterpated Disney princess?"

"I never said twitterpated," he grumbled. "And I was joking."

Harrison shrugged. "I don't think you're joking anymore, mate."

He sighed. "Okay, fine. Yes, it's nice to come home and have a home-cooked meal with a person who can hold an intelligent conversation. But other than that, the woman is driving me insane. I had the perfect bachelor pad and she is turning it into Mother Goose Central. I found a contraption the other day that I thought was supposed to be for some kinky game she wanted to play. Turned out the damn thing was a breast pump. I didn't know you could even pump a breast."

Cole was full out laughing at this point. Brooks glared at him and he held his hands up in defense.

"Sorry. I don't mean to laugh at your pain, but it's kind of nice to have someone else in the same boat for once. Just wait until she's further along. Then things start to get real interesting."

Brooks could only imagine. Then again… "I'm not sure she'll still be here by then."

Harrison frowned at him. "Why is that? You didn't cock it up already, did you?"

Brooks snorted. "Surprisingly, no. I don't think. But even if I haven't, this arrangement was never supposed to be permanent."

Cole frowned. "Have you two discussed her moving out?"

"No." He took another drink of his beer to hide his frown. The thought of her leaving filled him with emotions he didn't want to look at too closely. All he knew was that he didn't want her to go. "But we said we were only doing it to make sure she kept her job and things seem to be going well in that department. My place isn't set up for a baby. She's already almost halfway through her pregnancy. I'm sure she'll want to be settled in her own place before the baby comes."

"Sure," Harrison said. "Or you could make your place what she needs."

Cole pointed to him. "Now that's what I call a good idea."

"What do you mean?" Brooks asked.

"I mean," Harrison said, "you said your place isn't really set up for a baby. That doesn't mean that can't change. Go get what she needs. If your place won't work, get another place."

"Are you serious? It took years to get my place to the perfect pad of perfection that it is. Besides," Brooks said, shaking his head, "this is a temporary arrangement. I'm not going to change everything about my life to accommodate a woman who has no intention of staying in it. I like my apartment the way it is. It's one hundred percent suited to my needs and it's going to stay that way."

Harrison shook his head. "Well, not that my opinion counts, being the only single bloke in the bunch, but I think you're an idiot."

That made Brooks raise an eyebrow or two. "Well, damn, don't sugarcoat it for me or anything."

"Sorry," Harrison said. "But I find it idiotic that you've got it all and you are totally willing to throw it away."

The unfairness of that comment sparked an anger in Brooks that he tried to keep a handle on. He knew Harrison didn't mean anything by it and was probably even trying to help. But it pissed him off anyway.

"The only thing I've got is a full house," he said, throwing down his cards. "Pay up."

He grinned at the groans of his friends, though he knew the expression didn't reach his eyes. He'd never felt less like smiling in his life. He excused himself from the table for a minute and went into the restroom. If he was honest with himself—something he rarely did as it never ended well—he would admit that Harrison's comment stung so much because it was true. Only it wasn't because he was willing to throw everything away. He just had no choice about it.

They were getting along, great, yes, but she didn't want to stay with him. She'd never made any mention of anything of the kind. And no matter what he thought he wanted, he wouldn't be any good for her in the long run, either, let alone a baby. He'd never inflict himself on some poor defenseless child. Even if he wanted to, there was no way in hell any sort of relationship was going to work with Marcus in the picture. With him and Marcus playing Daddy One and Daddy Two? Marcus pulling his backstabbing snake routine every chance he got? Only with the baby in the middle? That kid would be in therapy before he hit kindergarten. And that was the best-case scenario. No way was that dynamic in any way, shape, or form healthy for the baby. Or anyone else.

So no, he wasn't throwing anything away, because he couldn't throw away what he'd never had. It didn't matter how much he wished the opposite was true.

He rejoined the boys and waited for his new hand to be dealt.

"So how are things going with Marcus?" Cole asked.

"Marcus?" Chris asked.

"Marcus Cassidy. The baby daddy."

"Wait, Marcus Cassidy as in *the* Marcus Cassidy? The guy who developed that designated driver taxi app and whose family runs half of the city?"

"No," Brooks said, tossing his chips into the pile with a great deal more force than necessary. "The guy who *stole* that designated driver taxi app after we developed it together and then used his family's money to lawyer up when I was too poor to do the same."

Harrison's eyes widened. "He's the baby daddy?"

Brooks stared at him and he whistled and threw his chips into the pot. "Damn. Brutal."

Brooks shrugged. "Doesn't make any difference to me."

"How can that possibly not make any difference?" Chris asked.

"Why should it? It's a fake marriage, remember? She's free to do what she likes." Though the thought of Leah doing anything, even speaking, with Marcus made Brooks's blood boil.

"Well, shouldn't you warn her that the guy is a snake?" Harrison said.

Brooks sighed and rubbed a hand over his face. "My issues with the guy shouldn't affect her. As long as he treats her decently, I'm going to stay out of it. She's got enough to deal with."

Cole's brows raised. "That's mature of you."

"Yeah, who knew I had it in me." He tossed down two pair. "Now, maybe you guys should pay more attention to the game before I walk out of here with even more of your money."

He grinned, grateful to the good hand for giving him a reason to change the subject. The truth was he didn't want Marcus within a hundred miles of Leah. But what choice did he have? The guy was the baby's father. He had more right to be in the picture than Brooks did, no matter how he felt about him.

He'd just have to learn to live with it.

Or move on.

# Chapter Fifteen

Leah looked in the full-length mirror, turning from side to side with a grimace. Brooks had been doing an amazing job at keeping up his side of the bargain, more so than she'd thought he would, especially now that Marcus was back and making a concerted effort to insert himself into Leah's life. It was something she could tell Brooks loathed, though he never said a word against Marcus.

Instead, Brooks picked her up from work most days, making sure to wave to the nuns when he did so. He came to the school functions, helping her out with anything she needed, and even stopped by the school a few times to bring her lunch. As far as anyone at school could tell, he was a loving, devoted husband and excited father-to-be. The hope and longing that never seemed to disappear crept back into her heart but she squashed it viciously. There was no room for nonsense like that.

Even if he were to do a total one-eighty and turn from the world's biggest bachelor into a happy, devoted family man, it didn't change the fact that Leah had no right to be by his side. She had no place in his world. He may have started with the same humble background as her, but that was a very long time in the past. He was a freaking billionaire, co-founder of some company that did things she didn't even begin to understand. He wasn't just part of some other world—he was in a whole different galaxy. And the gala they were going to that night only proved her point.

She had to make a good impression for him. Cole was still on paternity leave with Kiersten and the baby, so it was the first event where Brooks would be representing their firm solo. He needed to prove he could be the responsible face of the company, and Leah needed to play her part by his side.

She'd gone shopping with Kiersten to get a dress for the night. She had wanted to go to someplace like Nordstrom. Well, Target had been the first thought in her mind, but she knew something *that* off-the-rack wouldn't cut it. But apparently even a store like Nordstrom, which she could never afford on her own, was still far beneath the realm of the people they'd be seeing that night.

Kiersten had taken her to a couture shop where a woman had taken a one-of-a-kind gown and fit it to Leah's body. Her bloated, pregnant, bulging body. Kiersten had assured her she looked beautiful in the midnight-blue floor-length gown but it was far too tight for Leah's comfort. Not that she could show up in the baggy sweats that were all she wanted to wear after a long day at work, of course. But the revealing gown was something Leah would have never chosen for herself.

The off-the-shoulder neckline showed way more cleavage than she had even known she'd possessed. Though, a few months ago she *hadn't* possessed it so that could be why. Then, instead of flaring like the shapeless tent she wished it was, the material hugged her body, accentuating her baby bump and flowing to the floor in a river of sapphire satin.

The heels that she had to wear with the dress were another

problem. Leah loved a good pair of heels as much as the next girl and the shop assistants had kept them modest-sized just to be on the careful side. No one wanted her taking a tumble with the precious cargo she carried. But still, between her nerves and her changing center of gravity, Leah wasn't sure her heel-walking skills were up to par.

She stood staring at herself in the mirror, trying to think of an excuse that would get her out of going. But Brooks had done everything and more that he had promised. She had promised to help him at work, show that he could be a responsible, fully functioning adult that another responsible, fully functioning adult would choose to marry. She needed to suck it up and go.

The door opened behind her and Brooks walked in, stopping short when he saw her standing there. She watched his eyes rove from her feet to her head, his mouth slightly open, then met his gaze in the mirror.

"Is it all right?" she asked.

He gave her a faint smile. "Woman, you are so far from all right it's not even funny."

She frowned a little at that, trying to figure out what he meant.

He came up behind her, placing his hands on her shoulders. "You are absolutely breathtaking."

She released a breath she didn't realize she'd been holding. "Thank you."

She smiled a bit as he continued to look her up and down. The stark admiration in his eyes went a long way to build her confidence.

"You are missing one thing, though," he said.

She frowned. He pulled a long velvet box out of his jacket pocket and she couldn't help but smile, flashes of scenes from *Pretty Woman* going through her head. She opened the box, her heart skipping with excitement, only to frown down into the empty velvet interior.

"Really?" she said. She should have known he was going to prank her.

He grinned and held up his other hand from which dangled a diamond necklace with a teardrop sapphire pendant. "Kiersten told me the color of your dress. I thought this might match well."

She sucked in a breath as he placed the gems around her neck, her hand trembling slightly as she touched the beautiful stones.

"Brooks, this is incredible, thank you. You didn't buy this, did you? It's on loan or something?"

"Don't worry," he said with a wink. "It was on sale."

She frowned a little, knowing she couldn't accept something so extravagant. But before she could say anything else he pulled out another box from his pocket, much smaller this time, and placed it in her hands.

"So were these."

She opened them to find a pair of matching earrings—small teardrop sapphires dangling from a short string of glistening diamonds.

"Oh, Brooks," she said, but he shook his head and pressed a quick kiss to her temple.

"Stop complaining and put them on. Honestly, I've never met a more stubborn woman. A guy gives you jewelry, just smile and say thank you."

She smiled at him. "Thank you."

"See. That wasn't so hard, was it?"

She laughed and put the earrings on.

"Are you ready?"

She glanced at herself one more time and took a deep breath. "As I'll ever be, I suppose."

"Don't worry. It won't be that bad. And we don't have to stay long. Just enough to make an appearance, say hi to a few people, and show them that all their preconceptions about me were totally wrong and I am, indeed, the most awesome person on the planet."

She grinned. "So, we're never leaving?"

"Laugh it up, Mrs. Larson. You're the one stuck with me. For the time being, anyway."

"Lucky me," she said. And if she sounded like she meant that…well, she wasn't going to examine that too closely.

She picked up her velvet wrap and he took it from her, helping her drape it around her shoulders.

"Shall we, Mrs. Larson?" he said, holding out his elbow for her to take.

Those words always sent a little thrill through her heart no matter how hard she tried to stop it. A meaningless title she wouldn't have for much longer shouldn't affect her so much. But it did. Every time.

She took his arm and smiled up at him. "Lead the way, Mr. Larson."

Leah stood holding her glass of ginger ale, watching as some of the biggest movers and shakers in the city, hell, in the country, floated past her in gowns and tuxedos that probably cost more than she made in a year. And since her own gown fell into that category, she knew she wasn't just being catty. She had never felt so out of place in her life.

They had Bono on the stage providing the music, and she was pretty sure she had even seen Angelina Jolie chatting it up in the corner with a few of her celebrity friends. If Oprah showed up, Leah was going to call it quits then and there. Brooks, on the other hand, fit right in. Well, in some ways. In others, he stood out from the crowd. Literally. He stood head and shoulders above most of the men in there and his tux hugged every line and plane of his body as if it had been made for him.

She took a sip of her drink, hoping it would calm her stomach. She had no idea what to say to these people. They had absolutely nothing in common. But she'd better figure it out quick because a small group of ladies were heading her way.

"So," one said, a blonde with hair so elaborately styled it had to be a wig and boobs that Leah would kill for. "You're the one who snagged Brooks."

The woman looked her up and down, making it very clear what she thought about Brooks's choice. Leah might have been more uncomfortable than she'd ever been in her life, but that didn't mean she was going to stand there and let some woman walk all over her.

"Yes," she said. "Isn't he lucky? I'm Leah Larson." She held out her hand. "And you are?"

The woman blinked, mouth dropped open in a little *O*, obviously surprised that Leah didn't recognize her. And she should be—her face was plastered over most of the magazines and billboards in the city. Many of those pictures had been with Brooks, once upon a time. Leah knew exactly who she was, but she didn't have any intention of passing on that knowledge.

"You know, I've got to hand it to you," the woman said, her eyes glued to Leah's belly. "Classic strategy for a marriage trap, though risky with someone like Brooks. How could you be sure he'd stick around? He's not exactly the domestic type."

"Really?" Leah said in mock surprise. "He's been absolutely amazing, but maybe he saves that part of himself for people he really trusts."

The woman glared at her while her little followers started to fidget. They must not have been expecting a fight.

"If you say so. I think it's a shame a man as wild and carefree as Brooks has been…tamed."

Leah gave her a cold smile. "Oh, believe me, between us girls, there is nothing tame about my hubby."

"Talking about me again?" Brooks asked, smiling warmly at her and effectively ignoring the other women. He wrapped an arm around her waist and pulled her closer.

She looked up at him with a grateful smile. "Always."

"Good, my favorite subject." He gave her another squeeze. "How are you, sweetheart? I've been looking all over for you."

She resisted the urge to look surprised at the term of endearment. Normally, she would have said something about it, but he was obviously upset. No one else seemed to notice, but Leah could see it in the hard line of his mouth and in his dull eyes that usually sparkled with amusement.

She gripped his hand where it rested against her belly. "I'm fine, babe," she said. "I'm just getting to know your friends here."

"Not such great friends anymore," the blonde said with a little pout. "You haven't called me in ages, B. I've missed… talking with you."

Leah's hand clenched around her glass and she had to resist the urge to toss it in the woman's face.

"I'm sorry," Brooks said. "I didn't realize you were expecting a call from me. No offense, though," he said, with his usual teasing tone of voice. Leah noticed the hard note behind it, but she didn't think anyone else did. "I haven't thought about much else besides this gorgeous woman here." He pulled her in for a quick kiss and gazed adoringly down at her.

She was pretty sure it was all for show, but that didn't stop her stomach from doing a backflip or two.

"I've pursued this incredible creature from the moment

we met. She kept trying to ignore me, so I finally showed up at her door and whisked her off to a wedding chapel. It was the best day of my life. Well, so far," he said, placing his hand on her belly.

The blonde's face grew harder and angrier with every word. It was painfully obvious she had been one of the women who had chased Brooks hoping she would get to be Mrs. Larson.

The woman opened her mouth to say something else, but Brooks cut her short. "I'm sorry, Julie. Oh! Jenny, sorry. I hate to be rude, but we need to excuse ourselves. There are a few people I promised to introduce Leah to."

He gave them another forced smile and nod and pulled Leah away.

"I'm sorry about her," Brooks said, his jaw still clenched.

Leah shook her head. "Ex-girlfriend?"

"She was someone who wanted a lot more than I wanted to give her. She also believes far too much in her own appeal. We went on two dates and it was one and a half too many. And that's coming from someone with my questionable standards."

She squeezed his hand. "Oh, you're not so bad. You have your good points."

He smiled and kissed her hand. "Well, here's to hoping the good outweighs the bad."

He spent the next little while introducing her to almost everybody in the room. For the most part, everyone was polite and welcoming enough, although surprise and sometimes downright shock was evident everywhere she turned. But in a pleasant, almost relieved way. The uncomfortable laughter and confused looks melted into relief and acceptance once he introduced her as his wife, and the conversations often turned toward business ventures. As she'd gotten the impression this rarely happened for Brooks at these things, Leah was happy, hoping she was doing a decent job holding her own and propping Brooks up.

The rest of the evening had been going well enough that when Brooks needed to step aside for a moment to speak with a client she felt comfortable being left with a group of the other wives. They all seemed nice enough. Most were around her age, which was surprising considering that most of the husbands were a great deal older.

Two of the women wandered off rather quickly after discovering Leah had no interest in Paris Fashion Week or anything to do with the wonderful world of shopping. That left her with a sophisticated librarian-type woman and another woman in her late thirties, maybe early forties, who actually had a small plate of food in her hand. An anomaly in this group. Leah didn't think she'd seen anyone eating anything all night. Her stomach gave a quiet growl and she remembered it had been a few hours since she'd chowed on anything.

She tried to ignore it and turned politely to the librarian woman who had asked her a question. "I'm sorry," she said. "Could you repeat that?"

The woman blew an irritated puff of air through her nose, but asked her question again. "I asked what it was that you did for a living, dear."

"Oh," Leah said, happy to talk about something other than shoes and bags for the moment. "I'm a teacher."

"Oh really? Where do you teach? My husband is a professor at Yale. He's on sabbatical right now working on his next book, but I'm sure he'd be thrilled to make the acquaintance of a fellow educator."

Leah smiled. "I teach a literature class at a private high school in the city."

She could have sworn the woman's eyes glazed over. "Isn't that nice. I'm so sorry, will you excuse me? I see someone I must say hi to."

Before Leah could respond, she had excused herself and was making her way across the room.

"Don't mind her," the other woman said. "My name is Miranda. These affairs can be a bit cliquish."

"I'm beginning to see that. Apparently a high school teacher even at private school isn't quite on par with a college professor, actress, or trophy wife," she said with a laugh.

Miranda laughed with her. "You get used to them. And they'll get used to you eventually. It's nice to have some fresh blood in here, though it seems there is a new crop of wives or girlfriends every few months. Not that you need to worry about that," she said with a knowing look at Leah's belly. "I don't think I've ever seen a man so besotted with his wife as your husband. I knew once Brooks met the right woman that would be it for him."

Leah fidgeted, hating to continue with the lie when the woman seemed so nice and genuine. But this was a work function for Brooks and she was there to make him look better if possible.

"How far along are you?" Miranda asked.

"Twenty-three weeks," Leah said. "I have to confess I'm a little nervous."

Miranda waved that off. "Oh, don't worry. There's a learning curve to be sure, but you'll get the hang of it. And you'll have Brooks to help."

Leah glanced at her, not sure how to respond to that. "Well, I'm not sure how much of a help he'll be."

Miranda laughed. "Yes, the men definitely are better at helping create the little ones than they are taking care of them."

She nodded across the room at where Brooks chatted with a group of serious-looking businessmen. He seemed to be enjoying himself. He caught her watching him and raised his glass to her with a smile. Leah smiled back before she could stop herself and Miranda grinned indulgently. "It's nice to see two people genuinely in love for once."

Leah's gaze shot to her in surprise.

"Well, I better go round up my own husband. It was nice to meet you," Miranda said. "I hope I see you again. It's been nice to talk to someone real at one of these things."

Leah smiled at her, genuinely happy to have met her also. "It was my pleasure, truly," she said.

She turned her attention back to Brooks, enjoying the view until his face froze and his eyes narrowed. Leah looked in the direction where he stared and sucked in a quiet breath.

Marcus.

She frowned. Brooks had never been anything but polite to Marcus. Not especially friendly, maybe, but definitely not antagonistic. But the look on his face as Marcus came toward him made her think Brooks had been hiding a few things from her.

She hurried over to the little gathering just as Marcus reached them.

"There you are," Brooks said, kissing her on the cheek before giving a pointed look to Marcus.

Marcus stepped closer and kissed her cheek as well. "How are you doing?"

"Great, thank you," she said, a bit bemused by the amount of testosterone that suddenly surrounded her.

"Well, Marcus Cassidy," one of the men who'd been talking to Brooks said. He reached out and shook Marcus's hand. "I hear you're doing big things over in the Asian market. Good to see you back in the States."

"It's good to be back. I had some pressing family matters to attend to," he said with a quick glance at Leah.

She held her breath, but he didn't go into further detail. They hadn't discussed their situation and what they would say to people, but she certainly didn't want to drop the whole "I'm-married-to-this-guy-but-carrying-that-guy's-baby" bomb on the night when she was supposed to be making Brooks look good.

"How long are you in town?" the man asked.

At that, Marcus's gaze darted briefly to her again, but no one else seemed to notice. "I'm not sure yet. Several months, at least, though I'm considering relocating back to the New York office permanently."

"Well, they'd be lucky to have you." He turned to Brooks. "Larson, why haven't you dipped your toe in the Asian market?"

"Ah, Brooks here likes the comfort of home, I think." Marcus gave Brooks a friendly slap on the shoulder.

"Well, when I have someone so lovely at home, why would I want to be anywhere else?" he said, pulling Leah in for a quick kiss.

"Oh, don't be so modest," she said. "Brooks actually has several exciting ventures planned for the foreign market. I've been very impressed. Don't let that pretty face of his fool you. The Harrington Corporation wouldn't be where it is today without him, and Cole would be the first one to tell you so."

Brooks beamed down at her with a smile that made her wonder how long it had been since someone had complimented him on something other than his looks. She'd have to make a point to do it more often.

"Is that so? Well, we might have to keep a better eye on you," the man said, raising his glass.

"Yes, but you really need to move those ventures out of the planning stage," Marcus said. "You always were too cautious. You need to seize the day, be a risk-taker if you really want to make your mark on the world."

Brooks's eyes narrowed a fraction. "I think the Harrington Corporation has proven it is more than capable of making its mark. We've been a leader in this industry for the better part of a decade."

"Well, take it from someone who runs a company that has been a leader for the better part of a century, if you want to be in it for the long haul, you have to get out of your comfort zone occasionally."

"Oh, I have no doubt that the Harrington Corporation will be around for the long haul, as you say. Cole and I have every intention of making sure our company continues to be a leading innovator for generations, as your father and grandfather, who, I believe, are still the heads of your corporation, have done for the company you work for. Choosing to settle down in my personal life," Brooks said, glancing down at Leah with a smile, "does not necessitate settling in business. Harrington has a great many plans on the horizon."

"In addition to the amazing things you already have going," Leah said.

Marcus gave Brooks a tight grin and raised his glass to him. The other men chatted for a moment before taking their leave, but Marcus stuck around. A couple waiters passed with more drinks and food. Marcus grabbed a fresh tuna sushi roll and handed it to Leah. She politely accepted it, not wanting to hurt his feelings, but Brooks plucked it from her fingers.

"Pregnant women aren't supposed to eat sushi," he said, snagging her a stuffed mushroom instead. He leaned over and quietly had a word with one of the waiters who nodded and hurried off.

"Same old Brooks," Marcus said with an overly bright smile. "Somehow every time we are in the same room together, things devolve into some ridiculous rivalry."

"Because I don't want *my wife* to be poisoned?"

Marcus glanced around and then said, "You don't honestly think I'd do anything to harm *my baby*, do you?"

Brooks shrugged. "Maybe not on purpose," he said, pausing to take a tall glass of iced cranberry juice from the waiter who had just returned. He handed it to Leah who sipped it gratefully, a happy sigh escaping as the cool liquid slid down her throat.

"Keep them coming," Marcus said, throwing a fifty on the guy's tray.

Brooks shook his head. "But you can't seem to help trying to one-up me. You've been doing it since the day we met. And you don't care who you hurt in the process."

"Now, I think those are sour grapes talking," Marcus started, but Leah butted in.

"Excuse me," she said, searching for a way to break up the imminent pissing contest. "But my feet are killing me. I think I'd like to go home now."

"Absolutely." Brooks handed their glasses to another waiter.

Marcus took her hand. "Please don't leave on our account." He jerked his head at Brooks. "It's just a little friendly rivalry. We don't mean anything by it."

Judging from the tense look on Brooks's face, that wasn't quite the truth, but she didn't want to debate it right then.

She smiled and squeezed his hand. "It's not that at all. Or not totally that. I'm tired."

"Then let's get you home," Brooks said, wrapping his arm around her waist.

"I'll call you tomorrow," Marcus said, raising her hand to his lips.

Leah forced a smile. Marcus really was sweet, but having him in the same room as Brooks was a bit much.

Brooks gave him a tense nod and led her from the room and out of the building.

"You were wonderful tonight, thank you," he said as he helped her into the car.

She gave him a small smile. She hoped she'd been a help. She really did. But she couldn't help but be grateful that she didn't have to go to those parties every month. There was no way she could stand dealing with those people regularly. And she wasn't sure how great a help she'd been in any case. Certainly not with the wives.

A room full of models, tech giants, celebrities, business moguls, and other masters of the universe didn't seem all that impressed with a high school teacher, no matter how prestigious her school. And she didn't want to spend her life trying to impress them.

But for Brooks's sake, she hoped she had done enough. It would be nice, when all this was over, to know that being in his life had made it a little better.

"What's the deal with you and Marcus?" she asked.

He sighed. "Nothing. Just some old school rivalry. No big deal."

"Is this going to be a problem?" she asked. "Because he is the baby's father. I can't exactly tell him to get lost."

"No. Really, don't worry about it. Just guys being guys." He threaded his fingers through hers and kissed her hand.

Now, why did that make her even more worried?

# Chapter Sixteen

They were back in one of the most uncomfortable rooms Brooks had ever been in, only this time Leah was fully clothed. He tried to talk her into one of those flimsy paper gowns, but apparently one wasn't necessary. And she couldn't be talked into doing it anyway just for fun…or easy access. She also nixed the idea of him wearing one. Which was totally unfair. He'd rock the shit out of it.

She sat on the table lightly swinging her feet. A small thing, really, that she probably didn't even notice, but it had to be one of the most adorable things he'd ever seen in his life. Of course there was nothing adorable about the metal arms that were attached to the table. Those looked ominous.

"What the hell are those things?" he asked, pointing at them. "It looks like some weird alien dissection lab."

"You aren't too far off. Those are the stirrups."

"You mean like giddy-up-horsey stirrups?"

"Kind of. I put my feet in those and they hold my legs up so the doctor can examine me."

Brooks looked at how far apart they were and

envisioned the position that would put her in. Under normal circumstances, it might intrigue him. In the sterile medical environment they were in, it was nothing short of terrifying.

"Does it hurt?"

"Well, it's not the most comfortable thing I've ever done, but it's not that bad."

He stared at them a moment longer. "Nope, gotta try it. Scootch."

"What?" she asked.

But he was already nudging her off the table. He hopped up, put his feet in the stirrups, and stared at the ceiling.

"Okay, this is brutal."

"Well, I do try to be gentle," a voice said.

Brooks craned his neck up. "Oh, hey, doc." He gave him a little wave.

"I've found I usually get the best results when I examine the mother in these cases."

Total deadpan. Nice. "Sorry," he said, disentangling his legs from the weird metal torture devices and jumping down.

Dr. Petrosky waited while Leah climbed back on the table. "How are we feeling today?"

"Pretty good," Brooks said. "Had a bit of a big lunch so my stomach is hurting a little."

The doctor laughed. "I meant Mrs. Larson."

"Ah, right. I'll let her answer."

Leah shook her head, though she had that smile on her lips that she had when she thought he was being adorable.

"I'm doing fine, doctor."

"Good, good. No more spotting? A small amount after intercourse should be fine, but remember if it's bright red or you're bleeding through a pad, you need to come in right away."

"No," she said, her cheeks flashing crimson. "No problems."

She avoided his gaze. As well she should. They were cleared for sex? Oh, they so needed to have a talk when they got home.

"Well, let's take a look here." He got out the bottle of gel and pulled her shirt up enough to expose her belly. Brooks looked at it in fascination. He'd seen pregnant bellies before of course, but none up so close or as personal to him. Leah had been doing a good job of keeping covered up when he was near. For apparently no reason, at least not a medical one.

The doctor squirted the goo all over her belly and brought the little mouse-looking thing over. Brooks had been in the room the first time they'd done this, but he had been so stressed over the situation that he hadn't really paid attention to what was going on. The doctor moved the mouse over her belly and flipped a switch on the machine next to him. A weird whomping sound filled the room.

"Wow. Is that…" Brooks said in wonder.

Leah smiled and took his hand, drawing him closer to the bed so he could see the screen.

"That's the baby's heartbeat," the doctor said. "Nice and strong."

Brooks watched in awe for a moment as the doctor took various pictures of the baby, measuring its length, head circumference, and pointed out all the various body parts that they could see.

"And it looks like the baby is in a great position if you want to know the sex," the doctor said.

Brooks looked at Leah who stared back at him. He was dying of curiosity. He was the type who opened his Christmas presents early and then put them back under the tree, and who read the last page of a book first. He hated waiting, but it wasn't his decision to make. He shrugged at her with a smile.

She turned to the doctor. "Yes, I think I do want to know."

"It looks like you're going to have a little girl," the doctor said.

Brooks's heart punched through his chest. The rational part of his brain told him that this baby wasn't his. Leah wasn't really his wife. And in a few months, the whole charade would be over, but the rest of him wasn't really listening. It was listening to the magical *whomp whomp whomp* sound of the baby's heartbeat. It was watching the way Leah stared at the screen as if she could make out every feature of her baby. It was watching the intent way she absorbed everything the doctor said, soaking up every bit of information that she could.

It didn't matter if it wasn't really real because at that moment there was nothing else in the world that was *more* real to him.

The doctor gave them a few more instructions that Brooks didn't really hear, but before he left there was one thing he wanted to make triple sure of.

"So, we are fine to resume marital relations, correct?"

"Of course," the doctor said.

"You're sure it won't hurt the baby? She'll be okay?" Brooks was taking no chances of a repeat of last time.

"She'll be just fine. The baby is strong and healthy and so is her mother."

Brooks grabbed the doctor's hand and shook it on the doctor's way out. "That's wonderful news, thanks, doc."

Leah snorted from the table as she sat up and wiped a bit more goo off her belly. "Well that perked you right up," she said.

Brooks grinned and leaned over her with one hand on each side of the table so she couldn't escape. She looked up at him.

"Oh, you have no idea," he said. "Any particular reason you didn't tell me you had been cleared already?"

She chewed her lip. "I was nervous."

"Of hurting the baby?"

"Yes. A little. The doctor assured me all was fine, but still."

"And? Something else? Nervous about getting attached to me?"

He said it jokingly, though he found he meant it more than he'd intended.

"Yes," she said, raising her chin in the air. "This is supposed to be temporary and we agreed no sex for a reason. It complicates the hell out of everything. And we've already done it once. And it was…" Her cheeks flushed. "It was more than I expected. Doing it again…"

*Would be incredible.* Trying to keep from carrying her off right then and there took a lot more willpower than he thought he had. He got a grip and focused on Leah.

"I get it, really. But this relationship is already beyond complicated. Sex is kind of the major perk of being married, or so I've always been told. So why not make the most of it?"

She sighed. "Because."

"The only question that matters is whether or not you want me. Do you?"

Her eyes locked with his. "You know I do."

That look was like a sucker punch right to the gut. God, he wanted her. "Well, all right then. Let the rest work itself out on its own."

He leaned down to kiss her, but she backed off. "So, what, you want to go at it right here on the table?" she asked.

"Oh, yes, please." He trailed his hand up her skirt and over her thigh. She laughed and pushed against his chest.

"We're not having sex right here on the table. So move, you crazy giant. I need to get my shoes on."

He gave an exasperated sigh. Not that he had expected her to say yes, but it sure as hell would have been nice.

"Come on," she said. "The baby and I need some lunch."

He captured her before she could leave and gave her a tender kiss. "Your wish is my command. And then we go home for some dessert."

She just laughed. "You have a one-track mind."

"Hey, you knew this when you met me."

"Yeah, yeah. Now let's go eat."

He laughed and gathered her to him again, kissing her neck and holding her to him for a few moments. She could laugh all she wanted but if he promised her dessert, she was going to get dessert. Maybe twice.

A knock sounded and the door opened before they could say anything.

Marcus marched in, stopping short when he saw them. "Whoa, sorry there. Didn't mean to interrupt."

Leah gently disentangled herself, though Brooks wanted to hold on even tighter. Just to make a point, in case Marcus had missed it.

"You must have gotten the times mixed up," Brooks said, placing his hand on Leah's back to guide her out the door. "We were on the way out."

"I know, I'm so sorry," he said to Leah, ignoring Brooks entirely. "Here." He handed a large canvas shopping bag to her. "I've been reading up and the books all say that folic acid is important for expectant mothers, so I got you spinach and oranges and a bunch of avocadoes. And a few other things. I didn't know what you'd like so I grabbed it all. It's all organic, nothing but the best."

"Thank you, Marcus. That's sweet," she said, handing the bag to Brooks. She reached up and gave Marcus a kiss on the cheek.

"No problem at all. Nothing is too good for the mother of my baby. If there's anything you need—"

"I've got it covered," Brooks said, his fist clenching

around the straps of the bag. He didn't know what the fuck Marcus was up to, but having to deal with the guy day in and day out was going to get ugly.

It had been bad enough in college, but at least after Marcus had screwed him and Cole over, he'd disappeared. That wasn't going to happen in this situation, and Brooks didn't have a clue what to do about it.

The doctor came back in with a disk in his hand and looked between the three of them, obviously confused. That made two of them.

"I just wanted to give you the recording of your daughter," the doctor said, handing the disk to Leah.

"Daughter? It's a girl?"

"Yes," Leah said, beaming that bright smile that warmed Brooks to his soul. At least when it was aimed at him. "Sorry, I didn't know if you wanted to know, but..."

"We wanted to know," Brooks said.

"I would have preferred to keep it a surprise, I think, but no matter now."

Brooks shrugged. "Well, maybe if you showed up on time for the appointments..."

Marcus's eyes narrowed. "It couldn't be helped." Then he turned with that grin that Brooks was beginning to loathe and gave Leah another kiss on the cheek. "I hope she's as beautiful as her mother." Then he turned back to the doctor. "Can I get a copy of that?"

The doctor looked at Leah and she nodded. "Dr. Petrosky, this is Marcus Cassidy. He's...the baby's father." Her face turned the deepest shade of red Brooks had ever seen and he immediately drew her back to him, staring at the doctor and daring him to make some judgmental remark.

But to the doctor's credit, all he did was shake Marcus's hand. "Nice to meet you. Just stop by the front desk on your way out and I'll have my staff make you another copy."

"Thank you, doctor, I appreciate it."

The doctor waved at them and stepped back out, leaving the three of them to stare awkwardly at each other.

"We were on our way home so..." Brooks said, taking a step toward the door.

"I'll walk you to the car."

"I think we can manage on our own," Brooks said, but Leah shushed him.

"We can all walk together."

"One big, happy family," Marcus said with a grin.

Leah smiled back. Brooks rolled his eyes and started praying for the ground to open up and swallow Marcus whole.

• • •

Leah expected Brooks to pounce on her the moment they got home. Instead, he pulled her down to the couch, propped her feet up on his lap, and massaged them until she was limp and languid.

"Hmm," she said, trying to stifle a yawn. "If you were trying to relax me to get me in the mood, you might have overshot your goal just a bit."

"Seeing as how you spent the entire car ride home playing the head bob game, and not in a fun way, I figured you might need your rest first."

"I'm fine," she said, though her eyes closed before she could finish saying it.

He chuckled. "Get some rest, wifey. You're going to need it."

She woke a few hours later feeling a thousand percent better. He was right—she had needed that. She went in search of him. She had a stack of papers to grade and a lesson on Shakespeare to prepare but those would have to wait. Now that she'd rested up, an entirely different kind of need was making itself very evident. One it would be much wiser to ignore seeing as how it would do nothing but complicate the hell out of things. But that wasn't going to happen. It had to be the hormones, because she had never felt quite so…horny, for lack of a better word, in her life.

She found Brooks upstairs in the bedroom suite, at the corner desk where he had his computer set up. The chair was one of those cushioned rolling ones with no arms. Perfect.

"Hey there," he said, turning his chair around. "How was your nap?"

"Fabulous," she said, walking straight to him and straddling his lap.

His eyes widened, but he didn't object. Not that she'd expected him to. "Um, so it appears. Have any good dreams?"

She pulled his shirt over his head. "Not that I remember, no."

His forehead crinkled in a confused frown, but his hands came up to grasp her waist. She pulled off her own shirt.

"Whatcha doin' there?" he asked with his usual attempt at humor.

"I'm fucking my husband."

His grip tightened, and he sucked in a deep breath like he suddenly couldn't draw in enough air. She'd never been a huge dirty talker. Even if the thoughts were running through her head, embarrassment did a nice job of keeping it locked away. She had no clue what hormone combo had managed to amp up both her libido and confidence, but she liked it. And judging from the new, rock-hard bulge she straddled, so did Brooks.

He fisted a hand in her hair and dragged her forward to meet his lips.

That had probably been the first time he'd ever heard her really swear. She liked to save those words for when they were truly needed. Like now. When she needed him inside her so badly she could sob from sheer frustration.

He pulled away and she groaned. "Are you sure about this?"

She reached between them and fumbled with the button on his jeans, freeing him from the confines so she could wrap her hand around him.

"All right then," he managed to say while he liberated her breasts from her bra. He hesitated before touching them, obviously remembering how sore they'd been the first time. But along with everything else, the pain seemed to have eased up for the time being. And she wanted his hands on her.

She took one of his hands and pressed it to her breast, squeezing it to show him what she wanted. He didn't need to be asked twice. He took over, his thumbs rubbing across the sensitive peaks. Each touch sent a riot of electricity shooting straight through her.

For a brief moment, her self-consciousness about her growing belly nearly put out the flames. The last time he'd seen her naked, her stomach had only just begun to fill out. Now it was large and in charge. And yes, he'd seen the belly before, but not in a context like this.

But holding him in her hand as she was, she had all the evidence she needed that he still wanted her. And she needed him with an intensity she'd never felt before. She wanted to stretch it out, savor every second, but her body ached for him.

She scooted closer to him, angling her hips so his head rubbed over her entrance through the thin material she still wore. Her movements shifted her panties out of the way and he slipped inside.

"Wait," he said. "What about..."

"I'm already pregnant and you have regular physicals. I think we're fine."

She pressed against him, bringing him deeper inside and he groaned, grasping her hips.

He let her set the rhythm. She gripped the back of the chair and kept her mouth fused to his as she rode him. He kept one hand on her ass, griping her flesh, while the other tangled in her hair to angle her mouth so he could delve deeper.

Within minutes, that piercing pressure built to a crest that couldn't be contained. It crashed over her, dragging him with it. She slumped against him, her head resting on his shoulder, while she continued to shudder around him.

He stood, scooping her up in his arms so he could carry her to the bed. He set her down and stripped away the rest of his clothes, then leaned over to tug off her skirt and panties.

"This time, we take our time," he said, claiming her lips once again.

He made gentle, exquisite love to her until she begged him for mercy.

And then he did it again.

# Chapter Seventeen

Brooks walked into the room, looked around at a bunch of pregnant couples sitting there with their massive bouncy balls, yoga mats, plastic dolls, assorted baby equipment, and the most terrifying visual aids ever inflicted on a man, and prepared to bolt.

"Oh, what fresh hell is this?" he asked.

Leah laughed and pushed him into the room. "Come on, class is starting in a minute."

He ventured a little farther but stopped at the decapitated torso of a mannequin that had been cut away to reveal all the inside stuff. "Is that what really happens when you're pregnant?"

The mannequin had a baby in her belly, but everything else that was in there was squished up into the rib cage and behind the baby.

"Yes," Leah said. "Where did you think everything went?"

"I don't know. I never really thought about it. Not sure I'll be thinking about anything *but* that for a while now."

She grinned and towed him along until they passed a wall with a series of posters showing the various stages of labor and delivery, each one growing more horrifying than the last.

He grabbed her arm and pulled her to the side. "Let's get out of here. It's a total trap," he whisper-shouted at her. "If you stay, they'll make you do *that*." He pointed at the image of a baby halfway out of the birth canal.

She laughed and pushed him away. "I'm going to have to do *that* regardless. It would be nice to learn some techniques to deal with it. Now hush. Come on, let's go get a spot. The class is going to start soon."

He reluctantly followed her over to one of those yoga mats and had a seat. Leah sank to the ground much more slowly, her hand on her back. He helped her down and then pulled her back so she could lean against him. They hadn't really discussed the logistics of who would be where in the delivery room. In fact, now that Marcus had shown up—though he had yet to appear for the class despite promising to be there—Brooks wasn't completely sure whether or not he would be in the room. But, he wouldn't let Leah be in there alone and she needed a coach for the classes. Plus, he *was* technically her husband, so there he was.

The teacher finally showed, entering the class engrossed in a conversation with Marcus who actually had a pad and pen and was taking handwritten notes. Leah tensed slightly, but when he glanced down, she was smiling at Marcus. Perfect.

Marcus said something to the instructor and hurried over to them. "Sorry about that. I had a few questions I wanted cleared up so I came early and had a nice chat with the instructor. Don't worry at all," he said to Leah. "We'll be the most prepared parents in the delivery room."

He sat beside her. "Shouldn't I be the one supporting her? I'm the dad, after all. I assume I'll be the coach."

He'd been thinking the same thing only moments before,

begrudgingly. But with the d-bag sitting there demanding he hand her over, Brooks's stubborn streak kicked in. "She's already situated. And since I'm the husband, it would probably make more sense for me to be the coach."

"Oh," Leah said, her gaze darting with growing panic between Marcus and Brooks.

The instructor, who'd apparently been briefed by Marcus, came over. "One of you can support her and the other can coach her through the breathing exercises. And try to remember that you are here for her. She's lucky to have the support…if you're going to be supportive. Leave anything else at the door, gentlemen. This is about mommy and baby."

Brooks nodded, the unfamiliar sensation of shame crawling through him. He wrapped his arms around Leah and kissed her cheek. "Sorry. Mommy's in charge."

Leah shuddered but laughed. "Oh my God, don't ever call me mommy again."

He chuckled. "Got it."

Marcus scooted a little closer and took her hand, though he at least glanced at Brooks before he did it.

"I guess I'll handle the breathing then, if you've got the back support covered."

Brooks nodded. "Okay, though we should probably take turns with the breathing part. In case something happens and you can't show."

"I'll be there for the birth of my own kid."

"Didn't say you wouldn't be."

"Cool it, boys, or none of us will know what we're doing," Leah said.

Brooks bit his tongue and tried to pay attention, and was almost sorry he did. The instructor launched into a whole welcoming spiel about the wonders of childbirth. Brooks stared at her, his mind spinning. Who knew that having a baby was so complicated? You watch the movies and it seems pretty straightforward. Water breaks, woman screams, lots of panting, out comes baby. But all that panting was some super special breathing technique that he now had to memorize so he could coach his wife through it—because he wasn't leaving it up to Marcus—as she would be too busy being ripped apart at the seams to remember how to breathe. Wow. Talk about pressure. What if *he* forgot to breathe, too? They were so screwed.

Leah leaned back against his chest and looked up at him. He glanced down to see her concerned face. "You doing okay up there?"

"Yeah, sure, just fine." She didn't need to know that he was currently running through the thousands of ways he could screw this up and praying they all made it out in one piece.

Marcus's phone buzzed and he glanced down at it. "Shit, I've got to take this. I'll be right back. Cover for me for a minute, will you?" he said to Brooks. "I won't be gone long, I promise," he said to Leah.

"Bailing again," Brooks muttered.

"What?" Leah asked.

"Nothing."

She grinned at him. "Are you sure you don't want to go with him? I think they're going to be showing a video soon."

All the blood must have rushed from his face, because she sat up and turned to face him. "Really, are you doing okay?"

"Oh yeah, I'm fine. I didn't know there was going to be a video."

"Well, if you don't think you can handle it…"

"I can handle it if you can."

She shrugged. "Ten bucks you're out cold on the floor before the movie's half over."

"You're on. Just make sure *you* don't pass out." He eyed

her belly. "I'm not sure I can carry you out of here."

She elbowed him in the gut and he laughed and wrapped his arms around her. Only partly to keep her from hitting lower.

Okay, he'd deserved that.

Five minutes later he was pretty sure that bet was the only thing that was keeping him conscious. He kept his arms wrapped around Leah's shoulders as they watched the scariest movie he'd ever seen in his life. Every time the woman in the video screamed, Leah would flinch back against him and he'd hold her tighter. But there was a lot of screaming. Well, maybe it was more grunting and weird animal-like moans and growls. What. The. *Hell.*

At one point, she finally whispered up to him, "You're squishing me."

"Sorry." He tried to loosen his hold, but damn. That was some seriously twisted Tarantino shit going on up on that screen. Really, with all the technology available there *had* to be an easier way to get a baby out of a woman's body.

When Leah had first told him about Lamaze and what it was he felt silly even thinking about doing anything like that and had no intention of doing it himself. But after that film was over, he was pretty sure he needed it even more than she did. So when the teacher said, "Okay, pant like this... *heh-heh-heh...*" Brooks immediately sat down on the yoga mat, placed his hands on his belly, and started some deep breathing exercises.

He stopped when he noticed everyone staring at him. "What? Am I doing it wrong?"

"Your technique is great," the teacher said. "Except your wife is the one who's supposed to be doing the breathing. You're just supposed to be there making sure she's doing the right one and counting for her."

"Right. Sorry. Though, I really think there should be a

coach version of this."

Several of the other dads in the room nodded in agreement.

Leah shook her head, but she had that grin on her face that sent little bolts of warmth pinging through his heart. They switched positions, and he helped coach her through the series of breathing exercises. He had to admit after trying a few himself he did feel better. How it would possibly make Leah feel better when she was trying to push a human being out of her nether regions was something he still didn't understand. But, hey, if it made her feel better to learn, he was there for her.

Marcus wandered back in toward the end of the class, full of apologies, and took his place on the other side of Leah. The teacher went through a few final tips including info about something called an epidural. Brooks leaned over to Leah. "I think this is about drugs, take notes."

She rolled her eyes and slapped his shoulder but, hey, he wasn't kidding. If he was in her position, there was no way in hell he would be trying have that kid without a solid dose of anything they could give him.

"Natural childbirth would be best, I think," Marcus said. "Much healthier for the baby."

Leah and Brooks stared at him. Brooks finally said, "As Leah is the one pushing the baby out of her vagina, I think whether or not she takes drugs to make it less excruciating is up to her."

She held up her hand and he high-fived her.

Marcus held up his hands in surrender. "Of course, of course. I'm just trying to do what's best for our child."

"Don't listen to him," Brooks whispered to her. "They wouldn't let you do it if it was going to hurt the baby. I'll get you all the drugs you want."

She laughed and shushed him.

Then it was question-and-answer time. He rolled one of the huge bouncy balls over and sat on it. It was surprisingly comfortable. And bouncy. He might have to get one for the office.

Several of the women had questions about things like stretch marks and what they could do to prevent them.

"Well," the teacher said, "there's cocoa butter and some other special creams that you can use. Your partner can help apply them every night."

"I can do that," Brooks said to Leah. "Not a problem." In fact, rubbing her down with lotion every night featured prominently in several of his more erotic dreams. If she wanted to prevent some stretch marks, he was all over that.

Marcus's eyes narrowed slightly at that, but it wasn't like he could complain. Leah *was* technically Brooks's wife.

"It's also a good idea to begin to prepare your perineum," the teacher said. "This can be done using some olive oil, massage oil, or whatever you have on hand. And you lightly massage, like so." She demonstrated with her fingers.

Brooks leaned over to Leah. "I am totally down to help with that."

She giggled, but shushed him again.

"What about sex?" another woman asked.

"Excellent question, excellent," Brooks said, nudging Leah. "Take notes on this one, too, please."

Her face turned red, but he was sure it was because she was trying to hold in a laugh.

"Well, most of you ladies are in your second or third trimesters. I know for those in their second trimester in particular you've got those hormones kicking in. Most of you are probably starting to feel better, not so much morning sickness. It's something you should check with your physicians about if you are uncertain, but as long as your doctors clear you, you can have sex right up until you deliver. In fact, it's a good way to get labor started if you're a little over your due date. Just make sure you don't have intercourse after the water breaks. But up until that point, you should all be good to go. I know especially in that second trimester, sometimes those hormones can be pretty strong."

Brooks thumped his chest with his fist. "I'm ready and willing to take one for the team. You let me know. Anytime, anywhere. Those hormones hit, I'm right there for you. If I'm at work, you just call me right up."

He said that one a little louder than he meant, but most of the class was cracking up, Leah included, though she hid her face in her hand. Hey, they could laugh all they wanted. He was serious.

The class wrapped up and the teacher thanked everyone for coming. Marcus excused himself to go interrogate the instructor a bit more. Kiss-ass.

Brooks got off his exercise ball. "I'm getting a few of those for the house. They're insanely comfortable."

"You're killing me," Leah said, raising her hands.

He hauled her off the ground but kept her in his arms. "I wasn't kidding, you know. Creams, massage oils, hormones… I'm your guy."

She grinned at him. "I had no doubt."

He wrapped his arm around Leah's waist and nodded at the teacher on his way out the door.

"So, what did you think of your first Lamaze class?" Leah asked on the way to the parking lot.

"It was a bit more informative than I thought it would be," he said.

"And is that a bad thing?" she asked, laughing.

"When it comes to things like drug info and hormone surges, absolutely not. That fantastic video on the other hand…yeah that shit should come with a warning label."

She laughed again and he helped her into the car, struck

again by how normal this all felt. It was a strange balancing act. One part of him felt like he was on a plane ready to be pushed out without a parachute. He was out of his element, in over his head, and absolutely did *not* belong in a committed relationship with a pregnant woman. The other part of him felt complete for the first time in his life.

Marcus caught up to them and leaned into the car to say good-bye to Leah. Once the door was closed he walked over to Brooks's side.

"You know, you and I are going to have to come to an understanding about all this."

"Meaning what?" Brooks said.

"Meaning, I realize she's your wife, but she's having my kid. I'm not going away. You've always been a screwup. Finding out you got married blew my mind. Picturing you around a kid...*my* kid..." He shrugged. "Just making sure you know I'm not going anywhere."

"You've made it painfully clear, Marcus. But right now, I'm going home. With my wife. So, if you'll excuse us..."

Marcus held his hands up and backed away a couple steps before smiling and turning to walk off. Brooks took a second or two to get a grip on the fury rushing through him before he climbed into the car beside Leah.

The fact that Marcus wasn't wrong made everything that had come out of his mouth so much worse. Brooks had never seriously entertained the thought that he might want to be someone's husband and father someday. He *was* a goofball and a screwup, which was all good and fine when he was on his own. It made people laugh, so at least he could bring a little humor to the world. It was another thing entirely when it was a question of someone depending on him. That was a responsibility he had never wanted. And yet, there he was.

He and Leah still hadn't discussed what would happen in the near future, and he wasn't sure he wanted to. If he brought up the topic, it might set things in motion that he wasn't ready for yet. And with Marcus there, it made the dynamic even more complicated. The thought of dealing with that jag-off for the rest of his life made Brooks want to hop on the next flight for Nowhere and disappear.

For the moment, though, he would keep going along as though they were the happy little family they were pretending to be.

Maybe if he was lucky they could go on pretending forever.

# Chapter Eighteen

Brooks stood outside his apartment door staring at the knob.

Harrison leaned around his shoulder. "You've got to go in sometime, mate."

"I know."

Cole finally blew out a long breath. "Everybody move."

Brooks, Harrison, and Chris all stood out of the way to let the veteran daddy through.

"Have you ever been to a baby shower before?" Harrison asked Brooks.

"Seriously? What the hell is a baby shower anyway?"

"I don't think I want to know," Harrison said. "Is Marcus going to be here?"

"No, he had a big conference call or some other excuse. I didn't pay attention. Why?" Brooks asked.

Harrison shrugged. "This might have been one instance where having him around would have been handy, especially if it meant you didn't have to go."

The three men stood staring through the open doorway into an apartment that had been completely covered in pink.

Brooks looked at Harrison. "Hold me. I'm frightened."

Harrison snorted and pushed him inside. He and Chris followed behind Brooks, using him like a shield.

"The men are here," Izzy, Kiersten's old roommate and fellow lotto winner, said.

Brooks loosened up a little bit to see Izzy and their other friend Cass. He'd known them back when they used to work in the assistant pool at the office. Before they won the lotto with Kiersten. Since then they'd been traveling the world and having a great time.

Chris wandered over to Cass and gave her a quick kiss. Brooks and Harrison stared, mouths open.

"She's the one you've been seeing?" Brooks asked. "Why didn't you say anything?"

"Because I didn't feel like playing twenty questions with my personal life," he said. Cass elbowed him in the gut.

"I asked him not to say anything just yet. It's pretty new. I wanted to keep it between us for a while. But since we're all here at the shower..."

"Speaking of which," Harrison said, "I have a few questions. Do we shower at this shower? Or shower a baby? And if not, why the hell is it called a shower?" He glanced over at the other guys. "I know a few escape routes if anyone is interested."

"It's not going to be that bad," Kiersten said, coming up behind them. "And no, there is no actual showering involved, of a baby or otherwise. It's a party to celebrate the coming arrival where you shower the new parents with gifts for the baby. Basically, we'll be hanging out and talking."

Brooks, Harrison, and Cole all groaned.

"And drinking, for the non-pregnant people."

That made them cheer.

Kiersten shook her head and rolled her eyes. "Juveniles."

Brooks gave her a little bow. "I have been called much

worse, madam."

She laughed. "I know. By me. Last week."

He winked at her. "You know you love me."

Leah came in, her face lighting up at the sight of Brooks. "You came."

He leaned in to whisper in her ear. "I did. And so did you. Twice."

Her cheeks flushed deep red and he laughed, loving that he had that effect on her.

"Don't start with that," she said. "Or it won't happen again."

"Hmmm," he said, wrapping his arms around her growing waist and pulling her close. "You know you can't resist me."

She cuddled into him more, proving his point. Damn… too bad they couldn't sneak off somewhere and have a private party of their own.

"Okay everyone," Kiersten said, waving the guests over. "It's game time!"

"Run," Harrison said. "Run, now."

But there was no escape. Kiersten wrangled everyone together for a series of baby shower games, which, if Brooks was to be honest, he enjoyed. Not that he would ever admit that to another living soul.

He kicked total butt at the belly race. He and the rest of the boys strapped a ten-pound bag of flour to their bellies and raced around a small obstacle course Kiersten had set up on one side of the apartment. Brooks won, by a navel. Some of the other games he wasn't quite as good at, and one in particular terrified the shit out of him.

When Kiersten lined him and the other boys up in front of naked baby dolls beside a stack of diapers, powder, and blankets he was ready to bolt. Until Cole started in on how easy it would be for him to win since he was supposedly such an expert now.

"You going to let him get away with that kind of talk?" Leah asked.

"Hell no, baby." He rolled up his sleeves. "It's on."

He grabbed the baby powder and liberally doused his baby. And himself, by accident. And then Cole, on purpose. One good shot to the face, and Cole started sputtering and swearing and powdering Brooks back. He was not, however, diapering his baby, a fact he remembered when Brooks held his own baby up in triumph.

Sort of. He had managed to get the diaper on the baby, but it ended up being backward. And it may have taken him three or four tries, but hey, he did it finally. And the blanket… Well, who was to say that the way he did it was wrong?

Kiersten, apparently. And since she was the judge…

"The baby is covered," Brooks argued. "It should totally count. Take blanket, cover baby. As long as those two points are covered, I don't see why it needs to be done any other way."

"He'll suffocate," she said. "You've got his face wrapped up and his feet sticking out the top."

Brooks looked down at his baby doll. "Wellll, maybe he wanted to take a nap and it was too bright and it was just a little too hot so he stuck his feet out. Don't judge."

"Sorry, it's my job to judge. I declare Chris the winner!"

They all stared at him and his perfectly wrapped baby in surprise.

"It's like the damn barnyard all over again," Cole said. "How the hell is he so good at this stuff?"

"You guys act like it's hard," Chris said, glancing around at the other men who were almost entirely covered in powder with babies no reasonable person would deem properly covered.

Brooks looked at Cole and Harrison. "He's much too clean. I don't think he got any powder on his baby at all."

Harrison nodded. "We'd better check."

Chris didn't stand a chance. Three minutes later and he was seated on the sofa beside the others, powdered head to toe.

"At least they smell good," Kiersten muttered to Leah, who had to choke off a laugh when Brooks mock-glared at her.

Present time was much more fun. The women sat around in a group ooing and ahhing over each gift. The men on the other hand got to hang out in the kitchen drinking.

"Now this is my kind of game," Brooks said.

From the women's circle someone squealed, "Oh, how precious," and all the men said, "Shot!"

With the amount of times that phrase was being thrown about the room, they were all going to be too drunk to walk out the door by the time the party was over.

"Don't get too hammered," Kiersten called into the kitchen. "I've got a job for you boys."

They all turned and blinked at her like a bunch of meerkats watching for predators.

She pointed to a large box in the corner of the room sitting next to a tool box.

"Marcus couldn't make it, but he sent a gift. He said he'd put it together later, but since you are all here..."

"We've got it handled," Brooks said. No way was he letting Marcus show him up by getting the best gift in the room *and* being the hero that put it together, too.

"What is it?" he finally thought to ask.

"That's the crib," she said. "Get to it."

The men slowly approached the box like it was a snake poised to strike.

"Have you ever put one of these together before?" Brooks asked Cole.

He snorted. "Hell, no. I attempted once. For about five

minutes. Then I figured my wife and child would rather have me alive and sane, so I hired someone to come in and put it together for me. Plus, Kiersten threatened to divorce me if I didn't. Then she added a clause to the prenup forbidding me to attempt to assemble furniture ever again."

"Wonderful," Harrison said.

Chris frowned at it. "It can't be that hard."

The women chose that moment to start giggling at something. Brooks was pretty sure it wasn't related to their conversation. Well, maybe about eighty percent sure. Okay, fifty. They giggled again. Okay, they were laughing at them.

"Piece of cake," Brooks said.

Cole looked over at him, one eyebrow raised. "I hope you were referring to the fact that you want a piece of actual cake. Because if you were talking about this thing being easy to put together, then you really are out of your damn mind."

"Come on, guys, seriously. It's one stupid little crib. There are four of us. How hard can this be?"

There was blood before they even got the thing out of the box. Chris sliced his finger cutting the box open and was now sitting with it wrapped over in the penalty box. Well, really he was over on the couch with the ladies. But for their purposes, they were calling it the penalty box. And since Chris tended to be the Golden Boy who did everything perfectly, Brooks had more than a sneaking suspicion that the ass had purposely cut his finger to get out of setting up the crib. Brooks wished he'd thought of that first.

But the rest of them hung in there. Although there were two more cut fingers, a smashed thumb, and at least forty-three inappropriate curses before they had the entire thing unpacked and laid out in neat rows so they could see all the pieces.

"These instructions are in Chinese," Harrison said, throwing the paper at Brooks.

"Don't you speak Chinese?" Cole asked.

"Not well enough to understand those," Harrison said, flipping off the paper. "Besides, that's not really Chinese, it's English. Just really tiny print. And I don't speak English well enough to understand those, either."

"Look," Brooks said, pointing to the sheets of paper. "There are pictures. How hard can this be?"

"You need to stop saying that," Cole said. "Every time you do someone nearly slices something off."

Harrison yelped with a muffled curse and stuck his finger in his mouth.

"See," Cole said.

Brooks frowned at the incomprehensible instructions in his hand. "Come on, guys, we have to figure this out, or the poor kid is going to be sleeping on the floor." And Marcus would drop by to save the day and there was no way in hell Brooks would let that fly if he could help it.

There were a few more moans and groans, but the guys finally rallied and got the thing marginally put together. Sure, there were a few pieces left over when they were done, but it looked pretty decent.

"Get in it," Cole said.

Harrison shook his head and held up his hands, walking away slowly.

Brooks narrowed his eyes, trying to figure out what sort of sinister plan Cole had in mind.

Cole rolled his eyes. "I'm not trying to trick you. It's just a test. Make sure it's sturdy enough."

"I think the baby is going to be a good deal smaller than I am," Brooks said.

"Well, of course. That's why you climb in. If it will support your weight then it will definitely support the baby."

That sounded fairly reasonable. As did Harrison's suggestion that if they wanted to make extra sure it was sturdy maybe they should try it out with two of them. Which is what they tried to explain to Kiersten and Leah when they wandered over and found Cole and Brooks cuddled up together in the crib.

Brooks explained the whole thing and pointed at Harrison.

"It was his idea. He said he read an article about crib manufacturing that recommended using at least three hundred pounds to test the crib's safety. So we had to get two of us in here. Tell them."

Harrison just shook his head. "I don't know what they're talking about. I think they just wanted to cuddle."

Then he took off running.

Smart move really because Cole did an impressive vault out of the crib and took off after him. Brooks turned to Leah with a grin. "So, how are things going on your side?"

• • •

Leah tried not to smile. It only encouraged him. But really, it was impossible to keep it together. She laughed and shook her head. "We're having fun, though not as much as you're having over here apparently."

"Getting lots of loot?"

"Tons. Between this shower and the one the sisters and my friends at work gave me, this baby will be set for diapers for at least a year."

Kiersten laughed at that. "Try a month."

Brooks and Leah both blinked at her in surprise. She shrugged. "What can I say? They are little pooping machines."

Brooks opened his mouth, no doubt to make some inappropriate joke, but was sidetracked by a crash coming from the opposite side of the apartment.

"I'll be right back," he said, jumping out of the crib and

running full tilt to where his friends seemed to be doing their best to destroy his loft.

Leah just looked at Kiersten and shook her head. "It'll be like having two toddlers in the house."

Kiersten nodded. "True, but that could be said of most men."

She had said good-bye to the other guests before coming to check on the boys and Cass and Izzy helped her and Kiersten carry the gifts into Brooks's wine room.

"Is this going to be the nursery?" Izzy asked, looking around at the dark wood, humidors, and racks of wine bottles.

Leah shook her head and folded her arms, looking around. "We haven't discussed it. But it's the only available room in the house. Well, the only room with a door anyway. The master suite is upstairs, but down here is all open. I'm not comfortable putting my baby in a room filled with glass bottles full of alcohol. And Brooks isn't comfortable getting rid of any of it."

"Translate to mean, he flat-out refused?" Izzy asked.

"Yep."

"Why don't you guys get a new place?" Kiersten asked.

That would be the sensible thing to do. But again, she and Brooks hadn't discussed it. They hadn't discussed anything actually. They hadn't discussed whether they'd stay with the original plan and be done with the whole marriage thing once the peanut arrived or whether they were in an actual, *real* relationship now. Whether he wanted to be a stepfather. Whether he wanted Leah and the baby to continue to live with him once the baby came. How things were going to work with Marcus in the picture. *If* they'd work, because Brooks and Marcus, despite the polite smiles, did *not* seem to enjoy being around each other. All things that needed to be decided, and soon. And all things that Leah was afraid to discuss with him.

But her friends were looking at her, waiting for an answer, so she shrugged. “We haven't discussed that, either. I know he really likes it here.”

“Well, unless you're planning on strapping the baby to the pool table, you guys might want to think about getting a more kid-friendly place,” Cass said.

“I know,” Leah said.

Izzy and Cass gave her hugs before heading out. “You call us when that baby is born,” Izzy said.

“I will,” she said, walking them out.

“That was nice of them to come,” she said to Kiersten after they left.

“It was good to see them. It's been a while. They've been out jet-setting since we won that money. Although it looks like Cass may be ready to settle down.”

“Chris certainly seems head over heels for her.”

“Speaking of men who are head over heels, how are things with Brooks?”

Leah snorted. “Not head over heels.”

“Are you sure about that?” Kiersten asked, nodding over in the direction of the boys.

They were now standing around the kitchen counter with beers, but Brooks's gaze kept straying over to her.

“He can't keep his eyes off you,” Kiersten said.

“That's not love, that's hormones.”

“I thought you were the one who was supposed to have the hormone problems.”

Leah laughed. “Yeah, well he must be doing sympathy pains then. I can't seem to shake him.”

Kiersten raised her eyebrows. “Do you want to?”

Warmth spread through her cheeks but she shook her head with a grin. “Not really, no.”

“So it's going good then?”

“Better than I thought.”

"But..."

Leah sighed. "I wish I knew what he wanted. Where he wants this to go. *If* he wants it to go anywhere. Or if he even knows. And with Marcus always hanging around now, things are kind of...weird. Awkward. He's always doing nice things for me, bringing me stuff, and seems really invested in the baby. Though he does bail every time his phone rings. And don't get me wrong, I'm happy he wants to be so involved. I just wish he and Brooks got along better. And that I knew what the hell Brooks is thinking about Marcus and all the rest of this."

"Well, you know there's only one way to find out, right?"

She took a deep breath and blew it out. "Yeah, I know. Freaking communication."

Kiersten laughed at that. "That sounds about right." She glanced around the room again. "And you might want to make that talk quick. You guys need to figure out what page you're on so you can do something about your living arrangements. Or you're going to be tucking your baby in at night between a couple of wine bottles."

"Wine," Leah said wistfully. "I really miss wine."

Kiersten giggled. "Miss it all you want, but I don't think you want to have your baby shacking up with it."

"This is true."

She knew Kiersten had a point. The baby would be there soon, and they didn't have anything figured out yet. She wanted things settled before the baby came, and that meant she was going to have to have a conversation or two. Hopefully they went well.

She wasn't prepared to deal with the consequences if they didn't.

# Chapter Nineteen

"So, how's it going with the little lady?" Harrison asked, dealing out the cards.

Brooks glanced up and gathered his hand.

"That well, huh?"

Cole nodded at him. "What's going on?"

Brooks released a deep sigh. It wasn't something he'd planned on getting into. Poker night was his opportunity to escape from All Things Domestic. Although lately with Cole and Kiersten and their new baby, and Chris in a fairly serious relationship for once in his life, and Brooks sort of married with a baby on the way, a lot of their conversation had been taking a domestic turn.

Harrison, the odd man out as the only unattached one in the group, didn't mind, although he did seem to view them all as strange and pitiful zoo creatures that he enjoyed observing from the outside but had no intention of getting close to for fear they were contagious.

"Things are going great. When Marcus isn't around. Except he always seems to be around now," Brooks said.

"Well, that's a good thing, right? That he wants to be there for his child," Chris said.

"Sure. Except this is Marcus we're talking about. I don't know if he's there because he wants to be there for Leah and the baby, or if he's there to screw with me. He's got to be loving that he's the father of my wife's baby. He couldn't have planned this any better if he'd done it on purpose. I don't know how much longer I can deal with him."

"Yeah, well, seeing as he's the father, you're going to have to get used to him. You'll be the stepfather to his kid. If you stick around," Cole said.

"Can you imagine having to deal with that man, having to co-raise a kid with him for eighteen years? Hell, I don't think I could do it *without* another guy always trying to one-up me and get in my way. How am I supposed to do it with him pulling his usual Marcus shit? He's already got the whole biological father thing on me. He's been trying to work on Leah, too. And she doesn't know him like we do. All she sees is a charming guy, with old family money, who wants to be involved in raising their kid. Who wouldn't want that?"

Harrison shrugged. "Maybe she already has who she wants."

Brooks glanced up. "She hasn't said so."

"Maybe she doesn't know it's an option. Have you said anything to her?" Cole asked.

"No." Brooks shoved back from the table. "And I'm not going to."

"Brooks," Harrison said. "Look, I know it's up to you, mate, but you've been different the last few months. In a good way."

"Gee, thanks," Brooks said, cracking open another beer.

"He's right," Cole said. "You've been happy. And responsible. Hell, you have showed up for every single meeting, on time, and haven't made an inappropriate pass at anyone in months. And you've been *happy* about it. We're going to have to revive your mother next time she comes to visit. She won't recognize you. And we get it. A good woman will do that to you."

"Well," Harrison added, "they get it. I don't want it. I'm good the way I am."

Brooks snorted.

"But you," Harrison continued, "I don't think you've ever been happier. Who knew that being a responsible adult would be your dream come true?"

Brooks rolled his eyes. The only problem was they weren't wrong and that was all due to Leah.

"Look," Harrison said. "Yeah, it sucks that there is another guy in the picture. And it really sucks that guy is Marcus. However, she barely knows him. She spent one night with him. She's been living with you as your wife for the last six and a half months. Do you really think all of that time with you means nothing?"

Yes, that's exactly what Brooks thought, what he feared. And even if it *did* mean something to her, it didn't change the fact that Marcus wasn't going away. Brooks had no real rights in this situation, no place. He was her husband, sure, legally, on paper. But neither one of them had entered into the marriage with the intent of making it real, so in his mind it wasn't. It didn't matter how many rings he put on her finger. If she wasn't intending to be his wife for real when he did it, they didn't matter.

And the baby...the baby was hers. It terrified him to admit how much he cared for the little one already and she wasn't even here yet. What kind of a mess would that be to bring her into a world where he and Marcus were locked in some eternal rivalry? Being a stepparent would be hard enough. Having to co-parent with Marcus? Having Marcus always in his life...for decades? There was no way that would work.

Brooks shook his head. "Until she wants me for real, I'm going to go on assuming that our relationship is as it started."

"Well, maybe you should talk to her about it," Harrison said. "She might not know she has the option of keeping you. It's not like you have ever advertised that the whole wife and family thing was something you wanted. She probably assumes you can't wait to get rid of her."

The thought sent another spear of pain shooting through Brooks, but he ignored it. "It's probably better that way, anyway," he said. "Easier."

"Easier for who?" Cole asked.

Before he could answer, his phone buzzed in his pocket. He pulled it out and glanced down at the text. Then things got very strange. Like he was looking at the phone through a long tunnel. He could hear the boys in the background, but nothing they said really registered. The only thing he could focus on were those four words blaring at him from his screen.

*It's time! Come now!*

"Brooks?" Harrison said. "Did you hear me?"

"I've got to go," he mumbled.

He spun to find his three best friends staring at him like he'd lost his mind. They weren't wrong. He couldn't think of anything but getting to Leah. But once he did...*oh my God.* She was having the baby. Right now. It was coming right now. But he wasn't there. She needed him. He needed to get there. How was he going to get there? Oh yeah, he had a car. He needed to drive fast. He needed to go now.

"Brooks!" Cole said, snapping his fingers in front of Brooks's face.

Brooks blinked up at him while the world slowly came back into focus.

"Leah's having the baby," he managed to get out.

He'd never seen a phrase have such an effect on a group of men before. They all shot out of their seats and started scrambling around, throwing jackets at each other, patting pockets for keys, yanking phones out of pockets so they could start calling people.

"Let's go!" Cole called.

Brooks realized he was still frozen to the middle of the room. "Let's go! We have to go!" he said, suddenly filled with the energy of a dozen Red Bulls as awareness flooded through him.

He ran for the door with one thought blaring through his brain. He had to get to Leah.

Their baby was coming.

# Chapter Twenty

Brooks screeched to a halt in front of his apartment building. Leah was already standing on the curb trying to flag down a cab. "I'm here, I'm here, I'm here," he said.

"We have to hurry. I think the baby's coming now."

"Are you sure? It's three weeks early."

She glared at him. "Yes, I'm sure!"

He grabbed her around the waist and ushered her into the passenger seat of his car. "Don't worry. I've mapped out the route to the hospital. I can get us there in under ten minutes as long as traffic cooperates."

She snorted. "Oh sure, because traffic always cooperates, right?"

She said it with a smile, but the words still sent a rush of panic jolting through him. She was right. There is always traffic, but he couldn't worry about that now. He got her in and buckled her up and then ran around to the driver's side, jumping in and slamming the door.

"Where's your driver?"

"Out with the flu."

"Wonderful," she said through gritted teeth.

"It's okay, I've got this. We're all good. Don't worry."

She laughed a little, though the sound was strained. Then she took a deep breath and let it out slowly. "Okay. It's okay, Brooks. We probably have some time. It's my first baby. I've heard that they can take a while. So you probably don't need to ru—"

He slammed on the gas before she could finish her sentence. There was no way he was going to let the baby be born on the front seat. He was going to get her to the hospital if he had to drive on the sidewalk to do it.

"Brooks, slow down," Leah said, gripping the side of the car.

"It's okay," he said. "You just breathe. Don't forget the breathing exercises."

"I won't need to breathe if you kill us on the way there."

"Did you call your mother?" he asked.

"Yes. She's trying to get her plane tickets changed. She'll be on the first flight out. But she's not going to make it in time."

"Cole called Kiersten. They'll meet us at the hospital. Marcus?"

"I texted him after I texted you. He'll meet us there. Oooh," she groaned, gripping the doorframe until her knuckles turned white.

Luckily, traffic did actually cooperate, and they pulled up to the hospital in 14.3 minutes flat. Brooks jumped out and ran around to the passenger side, frantically waving at the orderlies who were coming to meet them with the wheelchair.

"My wife is in labor," he said. "We have a private room reserved for her. Mrs. Leah Larson."

"Yes, we've got everything ready for you. Let's get you inside," the orderly said, helping her into the wheelchair.

Brooks grabbed her bag from the backseat and threw his

keys at the valet who stood by waiting, then he hurried in after them. The next few minutes seemed a blur of activity, as the hospital staff got Leah checked in, gowned up, and situated in the bed. There wasn't much for Brooks to do except sit by and watch as they strapped all sorts of monitors and wires to her.

"Is all that really necessary?" he asked.

The nurse nodded. "The monitors help us keep an eye on mom and baby's heart rates. And it lets us know when contractions are coming and how strong they are. Speaking of which, looks like we've got another one coming on."

Brooks could have told her that without the instruments. Leah's fist grabbed the sheet and squeezed tightly. He pried the material from her hands, giving her his hand to grip.

"Squeeze as hard as you want," he said.

She panted through the pain, squeezing his hand until he had to bite his lip to keep from panting himself.

"That was a strong one," the nurse said. "This little one might be coming quicker than we thought. I'll check on the doctor."

She headed out. Brooks smiled when he spied an exercise ball in the corner. He pulled it over so he could sit more comfortably beside Leah.

"We have seriously got to get a few of these for the house. How are you doing?" he asked.

She lay back on the pillows and glanced up at him. "Probably about as well as you'd expect," she said.

He gave her what he hoped was a supportive smile and brushed her hair back from her forehead, leaning forward to kiss her temple.

"Not long now and you'll be holding your little girl."

She smiled up at him. "It doesn't seem real that she'll be here soon."

"Have you thought of any names?" he asked, trying to

keep her mind from the next contraction that he could see gearing up.

She breathed through it and then lay back, blowing out one last long breath.

"I have a couple," she said, waiting until her breathing had returned to normal. "Thought I should run them by you first, though."

Brooks glanced at her, hardly daring to hope that she meant what that statement implied. But before he could ask her to clarify, another strong contraction hit. She gripped his hand so tightly that he thought the knuckles might break. And he'd have gladly let her crush his bones if it saved her one ounce of pain.

Once it tapered off, he gently pried her fingers from his hand. "Those contractions are starting to come fast. I'm going to see if I can find the doctor or one of the nurses."

She nodded slowly, blowing air out through her teeth.

Brooks darted into the hall, frantically looking up and down the corridor. He grabbed the first nurse he could find. "My wife's contractions are right on top of each other. I think the baby is coming soon. Where's the doctor?"

"I'll have him paged, sir. Go back in with your wife. We'll be right there."

"Brooks!"

Brooks sighed. He'd half hoped Marcus wouldn't show, though for Leah's sake it was probably good he had. At least he thought so until he turned around and saw Marcus hauling the biggest teddy bear Brooks had ever seen.

"What the hell are you going to do with that thing?"

"It's for the baby. Nothing but the best for my little girl. Why? Did you not get anything?"

Brooks ran a hand over his face, his nerves frayed to breaking point, especially when Leah's groans of pain filtered out into the hallway. Marcus frowned and took a step in the direction of the door, but Brooks grabbed his arm.

Marcus looked down at his hand and back up at him. Brooks let go, but he stepped close enough that he could get his point across without anyone else hearing.

"Listen up, because I'm done with this shit. Today is about Leah. What she needs. No more of this one-upping bullshit that you like to pull. This isn't a game. We aren't in college anymore."

"Oh, I'm aware of that, but you don't seem to be. I know you think I screwed you over back then—"

"You did screw me over!"

"It was ten years ago, Brooks. Let it go already. Shit. You hold a grudge like a sixteen-year-old girl."

He wasn't wrong, which pissed Brooks off to no end. However, it wasn't the important point at the moment so Brooks tried to focus.

"This has nothing to do with you stealing that app out from under me or anything else that has happened in the past. It has everything to do with your obsessive need to compete with me. Leah and the baby aren't some sort of prize to be won or weird leverage for you to use to get at me, but that's the way you've been treating them and it's going to stop. Now."

"I think your perspective is a bit skewed. That's *my* baby she's having in there, not yours. I'm not the one trying to use them for leverage. I'm just trying to be a part of my kid's life, something you are making extremely difficult."

"She's my *wife* and that makes this situation a little more complicated than that. And I've done nothing but make sure you were included in all this, despite my feelings on the matter."

"Your wife, huh? Yeah, well I've heard more than a few credible rumors that the whole marriage situation isn't exactly what it seems to be, so I wouldn't go throwing that word around too much, acting like it gives you the right to call the shots."

"Both of you shut up and get in here!" Leah called out.

Brooks could have stapled his mouth shut. The last thing he wanted was for her to hear all that.

"Shit," he muttered, running a hand through his hair.

Marcus snorted and pushed past him into the room.

Before either could say a word, Leah held up a hand. "You two are ridiculous. Yes, we are in a complicated situation, but I'm busy at the moment and could use a little support right now. If you can give that to me, great. Take a spot on either side, and keep your mouths shut. If you can't, there's the door. I'll deal with you when I'm done pushing a freaking human being out of my body. Okay?"

Brooks immediately took her hand and leaned over to kiss her forehead. "You got it. I'm sorry."

"Don't be sorry, just be quiet."

He grinned at her. "Yes, ma'am."

"What about you? You have any issues?"

Marcus took her other hand. "Not for the moment, no."

"Good, now both of you shut up, because another one is starting."

She gripped their hands hard and sat forward, curling in around the pain.

Brooks rubbed her back. "The doctor is on his way," he said, hoping that that was true.

She nodded, but was too far gone in the middle of a contraction to say anything.

Thankfully the doctor entered the room not long after.

"Greg, hi," Brooks said, disengaging from Leah just long enough to shake his hand.

"Well, let's see what we have here," the doctor said, grabbing a stool and moving to the end where all the action was happening.

Brooks took up his position back near Leah's head,

smoothing her hair back and holding her hand as she breathed through yet another contraction. Marcus stood silently, lending his support but looking on with a sort of horrified fascination that was almost comical.

"Looks like you're ten centimeters and ready to go. That was fast, especially for a first baby."

"Fast is good, right?" Brooks asked.

"It's not good or bad," the doctor said. "Babies come in their own time, but it looks like this one is eager to make her mother's acquaintance."

They got Leah's legs propped up, with a nurse holding each leg. Brooks positioned himself behind her, helping to support her back, and Marcus stayed up front, helping to coach her through her breathing.

"All right, we're going to push now, okay?" the doctor said.

Leah nodded, trying to pant through the contractions.

"When I tell you to push, you're going to push for a count of ten."

Leah nodded again, and the doctor began to count.

"All right, now give me a good push. One…two…three…four…five…six…seven. Almost done, and good. Now rest just a moment."

They went through the same thing several more times as Leah strained to push her baby into the world. Brooks stood by watching with awe as this incredible woman labored to give birth. It made him want to pick up his phone and call his mother and apologize for everything he'd ever put her through. He'd seen the tapes, been to the classes with Leah, even read a dozen books when no one was looking, but nothing had prepared him for the real thing.

And then Leah finally slumped back against him with a deep sigh. Brooks looked down at her in concern until she smiled up at him with a triumphant glow.

There was some jostling around down at the other end while the doctor and nurses situated the squirming, squalling, little bundle of gooey baby. Who was then promptly laid on Leah's chest.

She smiled and laughed, using the end of the blanket to wipe some weird goo from the baby's eyes.

Brooks reached out a hesitant hand but glanced at Marcus and pulled back. Her father should get to see her first. Leah smiled up at him and then at Marcus who leaned over for a closer look. The baby was sticky, purple, covered in all kinds of weird and disgusting things…and she was the most beautiful thing Brooks had ever seen.

Except for her mother.

He leaned down and gave Leah a long, lingering kiss. "You blow me away," he said, so full of amazement and overwhelming love for his two girls that he could barely speak.

A nurse tapped him on the arm. "Do you want to cut the cord, Dad?" She held out a pair of scissors.

He glanced at Leah, startled. Her gaze darted between the two men. Brooks shook his head before Marcus could say anything.

"He's the father."

The nurse looked a little confused, but handed the scissors to Marcus. Brooks stepped back, suddenly feeling like he was intruding on someone else's family moment.

Marcus cut the cord and beamed down at Leah and their baby. Brooks watched it all, his heart swelling with so many emotions he couldn't begin to process them all.

The nurse took the baby to get her cleaned up and, after a few moments, gave her back to Leah. Marcus snapped a few pictures and then stepped to the side for a moment to call his parents.

The doctor had kept working, delivering the afterbirth

and getting Leah somewhat situated. Brooks went back to her side, sitting on the edge of the bed so he could put his arm around her shoulders as they gazed down at the baby together.

"Isn't she beautiful?" Leah asked, beaming up at him.

He stared down at the wrinkly little thing that still needed a good bath and looked like she'd had a very rough day. "I've never seen anything more beautiful in my life," he said, his heart swelling with love and pride.

The doctor shook both of their hands and they thanked him profusely.

Once they were alone, Brooks stared down at the new little life Leah had brought into the world. It didn't seem possible that one minute she hadn't been there, and now here she was. Beautiful. Tiny. Helpless. Completely dependent on them for life-giving care and sustenance.

He glanced at Leah, wondering if her throat had started squeezing shut in panic, but she still stared at her daughter with total and utter awe.

He slid down beside them on the bed, wrapping an arm about Leah's shoulders, and she settled against him. After a few moments, her body relaxed, though her hold on the baby remained steady. She really should rest. But that would require him either calling a nurse in to put the baby back in her bassinet, or doing it himself. Of the two options, calling the nurse definitely seemed the best course of action. Cowardly, maybe. Okay, totally. And completely unnecessary as he, a fully grown adult, sat there perfectly capable of transferring seven pounds of cuteness into a bassinet not even three feet away. Theoretically capable.

He stared down at the baby, trying to figure out where exactly he should place his hands that would support every squishy, cuddly inch. Though, hell, her little head fit in the palm of his hand. If he just slipped it beneath her...

He carefully slid his hand and forearm beneath the baby but Leah jolted awake.

"It's okay," he said. "I'm just taking the baby so you can rest."

"Thank you," she whispered, giving the baby a kiss on the forehead before relinquishing her.

Leah had fallen back asleep before Brooks had fully sat back up. Not that he could blame her. She'd just produced an entire human being. The woman had earned some sleep. Though that left him with the little one. He stood slowly, careful not to jostle her, and for a moment just stood with her solid warmth bundled in his arms. His heart swelled with overwhelming emotion, stunning in its intensity. How could he possibly feel so strongly for a little creature who hadn't even been in the world a few hours ago? Who technically had no ties to him, other than through her mother? It hadn't occurred to him he'd feel so strongly for her. Well, that he'd feel for her at all, really. He'd been concerned for her welfare in a vague sort of way, but now that she was here…

She made a gurgling sound and blew a bubble and he grinned down at her. "All right, little lady. I think you could probably use some rest, too."

He laid her with as much care as possible in her bassinet, sliding his hands out from under her body with infinite care so he didn't accidentally bruise anything. How was he supposed to help take care of something that felt as though she'd break if he sneezed too hard in her direction? Not that he knew the first thing about taking care of babies.

Maybe he should have paid more attention in those classes Leah had been dragging him to. Or read more of the books she had scattered all over the apartment. There was no way he'd be able to pull this off without making some horrible mistake. He was the last person who should be caring for a baby.

She deserved better. They both did.

And then Marcus walked back in, arms full of flowers and a proud, beaming smile on his face. And for the first time, Brooks considered that maybe Marcus really was the best man for the job. Maybe he hadn't been pulling his same old rivalry shit, but was just trying to do the best he could for Leah and his baby. *His* baby. Not Brooks's. Brooks really had no place in that room at all.

He watched Marcus lean over the bassinet, face full of the same wonder that Brooks had felt as he'd gazed down at the baby. He looked at Leah, sleeping like an angel in the bed beside her little girl.

And then he turned and walked out.

• • •

Leah kept glancing at the door, waiting for Brooks to come back in. She'd woken just as he'd turned to leave and the expression he'd had when he left…it made her want to jump out of her bed and track him down.

She shifted her weight and sucked in a breath at the twinge from all the tender bits. Okay, maybe jumping out of bed was a tad extreme. The baby made a cute little squeaking sound and Leah smiled.

Marcus came closer, gazing down at the baby. "She's so tiny."

Leah held her out. "Would you like to hold her?"

"Oh, um…"

"It's okay." Leah held her out and Marcus took her carefully. "Just support her head," she said, giving him some direction.

Seeing him holding the baby unsettled her. Of all the strange emotions she'd been riding lately, this might be the strangest. Watching Marcus hold her child. Their child. She needed to wrap her head around that.

The turmoil in her heart roiled over Brooks suddenly walking out. She knew he was probably in the next room, maybe trying to be the bigger man and let Marcus have some time with the baby. But she couldn't help feeling there was something more to it than that. All she knew was that he'd left, and he hadn't looked like he was going to come back. Physically, yes, she knew he wasn't far. But emotionally…she couldn't get that look on his face out of her mind. Something had changed in him the moment he'd stepped back so Marcus could cut the baby's cord, something that made her heart ache with promised pain.

At the same time, watching Marcus cradling their newborn daughter touched her in a way she hadn't thought possible. He stared at her in awe, in much the same way Leah imagined she looked when she gazed at her baby. He cuddled her close and gave her a kiss on her forehead, pausing to inhale the new baby scent.

"Settled on any names yet?" he asked.

Leah gave him a small smile and shook her head. "Not yet."

She didn't mention that she hadn't decided because she and Brooks hadn't been able to agree on anything. And because she hadn't been sure what last name to give her.

"Did you have any ideas?" It was only fair to ask. He was the baby's father after all.

"Oh no," he said. "Anything you pick will be fine."

They sat in somewhat uncomfortable silence for several minutes. Most of Marcus's attention stayed on the baby. He drew a finger down her little face, examined each toe and finger, smiled when she grasped his thumb with a surprisingly strong grip.

"She's strong," he said.

Leah beamed with pride. "Yes, she is."

"And beautiful like her mother."

Leah's cheeks warmed. It was a sweet thing to say, but she couldn't help wanting Brooks to be the one saying it.

The baby began to fuss a little, and Marcus leaned over to hand her back.

"I think she might be hungry," Leah said.

"Oh," said Marcus. "Would you like me to leave?"

"No, it's fine," Leah said.

She pulled one of the swaddling blankets over her shoulder to block his view of her and the baby, even though he'd seen it before. And really, after all the poking, prodding, and fondling she'd had over the last several months, culminating in the free-for-all at the birth when it seemed like half the hospital had been digging around in her nether regions, she didn't care who saw her boob or anything else anymore. But she felt a little more comfortable covering up since she was still new at the whole breastfeeding thing and found it easier to let it all hang out there until the baby latched on.

"So," she said, once she got the baby situated. "I guess we've kind of run out of time to figure out how this whole situation is going to work."

Marcus gave a little laugh, and played with the hat in his hands. "Yeah. This is…it's…"

Leah laughed also. "A bit complicated."

"That's definitely the word for it."

"I know you and Brooks don't exactly see eye to eye on most things…"

"Don't worry about me and Brooks. We'll figure all that out, too. Just have a little history to get over, that's all."

Leah tried to stifle a yawn. It had been a long week. She hated having things between the two men in her life so unsettled but…she really just wanted to curl up and sleep.

Marcus, bless him, picked up on that.

He stood and looked down at them for a moment longer.

"I think I'll go and let you get some rest," he said. "But I won't go far. And…thank you. For my daughter."

His voice cracked a little on the last word and Leah started to get a little choked up herself. He leaned down and gave them both a kiss on the forehead and then left quietly, closing the door behind him.

Leah gazed down her daughter for several moments. "Well, little peanut," she said. "Now what are we going to do?"

# Chapter Twenty-One

The baby made a sound that Leah could only describe as a half-strangled chipmunk squawking at the top of her squeaky little lungs.

It had been nearly a week and that sound still startled and confused Leah for a second, though she responded to it before she was even fully awake every time.

Brooks rolled over and put the pillow over his head with a groan and Leah laughed.

"I'll get her," she said.

Brooks mumbled something half-hearted about getting up, but she ignored him. It had been a very long night. The baby, who usually could run for perfect textbook baby of the year, had decided she'd had enough of behaving and refused to sleep unless being held, fed, or generally coddled. Not that Leah minded. Her little princess had captured her heart from the moment she'd entered the world and pampering her was generally a pleasure. Doing so on just a few hours sleep…not as much fun.

For Brooks…yeah, even less fun. He'd been surprisingly

game to help out with everything baby-related. Though he typically needed so much reassuring it was easier to do it herself. And despite his assurances, she knew they were cramping his lifestyle. After he'd left the hospital right after the baby's birth, Leah hadn't been at all sure they'd be returning to his apartment. But he'd been there when she'd woken. And when it had been discharge time, he'd gathered them up and brought them home.

Still, things couldn't go on as they were. They were going to have to figure everything out. Time was up. The peanut had arrived and she needed a stable home. Somewhere. And Leah grew less and less sure that that *somewhere* should be with Brooks. It had been bad enough having a pregnant woman under his roof, but with the baby there now, and Marcus dropping by almost every day…

Leah sighed and scooped up the baby, taking her out to the couch so she could feed her without disturbing Brooks more than necessary.

The sun shone brightly and Leah blinked sleepily at the clock. Ten in the morning. She stifled a yawn and got the baby settled into nursing. Their hours were completely messed up.

She looked down at the baby. "You need to learn the difference between day and night, my little love," she said. She ran a hand over the baby's soft downy hair. "And we really need to find you a name. Lucy…are you a Lucy?"

The baby didn't react.

"Emma? Charlotte? We could call you Charlie for short."

The baby kept right on nursing.

"I still say you go with something unusual. Make her stand out in the crowd. Like…Chadwick," Brooks said, rubbing a hand over his face as he stumbled in the direction of the coffee pot.

Leah chuckled. "I'm not calling her Chadwick."

"You could go full-on celebrity and call her Rainbow

Unicorn Dust. Or Poppyseed Cornbread."

"Oh, those are lovely," she said, trying not to laugh too hard or she'd dislodge little Unnamed One. "I'm a terrible mother, aren't I? I mean, she's been here almost a week and I still haven't named her. What kind of mother can't name her own child?"

Brooks carried his coffee over to her and leaned down to kiss her head. "The kind who loves her child so much she wants to wait until she has the perfect name. Take your time. Her Majesty isn't going anywhere."

Leah's laugh turned to a gasp when Brooks turned to navigate around the couch but got tangled up in the straps of the diaper bag lying near the end. His body went one way, his legs stayed with the diaper bag, and in a move truly worthy of a hero movie, he twisted in time to keep his hot coffee from splattering Leah and the baby, tossing it instead over his other shoulder toward the pale white wall behind him. He went down hard. Let out a grunt of distressed air. And then lay perfectly still.

"Ow."

Leah put the baby in the bassinet they kept near the couch and hurried to him.

"Are you okay?"

He blinked up at her. "That depends on your definition of okay."

Her lips twitched. "Anything broken?"

He frowned. "Not that I'm aware of."

"Need help up?"

He shook his head. The movement brought his newly coffee-splattered wall, and the painting centered on it that now sported a new brown splotch, to his attention.

Leah shrugged. "I kind of like it. It's like a big abstract mural or something with the coffee adding a new dimension to the painting that carries right off the canvas."

He snorted. "Yeah. I'm sure the new design will make an original Jackson Pollock worth even more."

Leah's mouth dropped open. "Oh my gosh, is it…"

He waved her away. "Don't worry about it. Hopefully it can be cleaned or restored. The more pressing problem is finding a place for all this stuff," he said, sitting up and rolling his shoulders. "Or get rid of most of it. Surely something that little," he said, pointing in the direction of the baby, "doesn't really need this much."

Leah glanced around. He wasn't wrong about the stuff everywhere. The apartment had been redecorated in wall-to-wall baby gear. Brooks's once seductive bachelor pad had turned into Baby Central and no matter what he said, she could tell he wasn't all that thrilled with the changes. But he was wrong about whether she needed it all. There were quite a few things she didn't have that she'd like to but hadn't gotten because there was nowhere to put it.

And it wasn't because his apartment wasn't big enough. The place was huge. But an industrial loft, no matter how jazzed up, wasn't a great spot for a baby. At least not if they were going to keep the pool table and poker table and bar and gaming center and all the other non-baby-friendly crap he had and refused to get rid of. They were really going to have to bite the bullet and discuss their arrangements. If they were going to make them permanent. Or try to. Or if they were going to start looking for another place. A place where the baby stuff could go in the baby's room instead of being strewn haphazardly about where anyone could trip and break their neck.

She wouldn't even think about when the baby became mobile. The entire apartment would transform into a death trap—if they were even there that long.

The baby was born. Technically, their little charade should be coming to an end. Brooks won the marriage pool. He'd stuck it out through Baby Day, but they hadn't discussed what happened next, and she wasn't sure what he wanted. He hadn't asked her to go.

But he hadn't asked her to stay, either.

The buzzer sounded and Leah jumped and ran for the baby, who immediately began to wail. Brooks hauled himself up from the floor and hurried to answer the intercom.

She bounced the baby who hiccupped a few times and subsided back into sleep.

"It's Marcus," he said, opening the door. "I'll be in the other room."

He disappeared into the wine room and closed the door before Leah had a chance to say anything.

She took a deep breath, trying to force the hurt and frustration back into its dark little corner. Marcus and Brooks had called a sort of truce for the birth of the baby, but the moment they'd come home, the truce had ended. Now things were deteriorating day by day. It had only been a week and things had gone downhill to the point that Brooks wouldn't stay in the same room as Marcus if at all possible. How the hell were they supposed to make a functional family unit for the baby if the men couldn't even be in the same room?

Marcus came in and looked around, relaxing a little when he saw it was only her.

"How are you lovely ladies this morning?" he asked, handing her an iced tea that she gratefully accepted and nearly downed in a couple large sips. Nursing was thirsty work.

"We're good," she said, though her gaze flickered to the wine room.

"No Brooks this morning?"

Leah gave him a tight smile. "He's home, just…busy."

Marcus sighed and sat down. "I wish you'd let me hire a nanny. Even part time. It would give you a little break, a little extra help. I'd be here more, but with these mergers getting ready to go through…"

"I totally understand. And it's sweet of you, really. But I'm fine. I promise. We just haven't found our groove yet."

"Well, if you change your mind, I've got a handful of excellent choices for you to look at. Say the word."

"I will," she said. She really did appreciate the offer, but there was no need to hire a nanny, at least not until she went back to work. Until then, she'd manage on her own.

"Okay, I've got paperwork for insurance and the trust fund I've set up for little Miss Perfect here. But we really have to settle on a name because eventually we'll need it for the legal documents. Right now we can go with offspring, I suppose, but it's not ideal."

Leah spaced out a little as Marcus droned on about very important details she really needed to be paying attention to. But every time he'd make a statement she'd think about how Brooks would react and how she could minimize the antagonism between them. Frankly, the whole damn thing was exhausting.

"Marcus," she said, holding out a hand to interrupt him. "All this is great, really. But do you mind if we continue later on? The baby just woke up and I haven't showered yet and—"

"Not a problem. We can do this whenever. Sign these two real quick," he said, laying a couple documents in front of her. "These will get her insurance going and gives you access to a few funds I'm setting up."

She didn't bother protesting any more. Just signed on the dotted line.

"Excellent. All right, my beautiful girls." He leaned over and gave them both a kiss. "I shall return later."

Leah smiled and waved as he left, and then slumped back against the couch, cradling her baby and waiting for Brooks to come out and start bitching about Marcus like he always did.

What in the world was she going to do with all the baby daddy drama?

# Chapter Twenty-Two

Brooks sat in his armchair and leaned his head back, trying to process everything. He'd heard every word. The wine room had a door, but the walls cordoning off the room didn't reach all the way to the ceiling. Sound had no problem carrying. Brooks had never really paid attention to it before. He wished he had or he'd have excused himself and gone outside. Where he couldn't hear Marcus the Hero marching in to save the day, offering his undying support. Money, insurance, nannies, anything she needed.

It was only right for him to do so and Brooks should be glad he was a stand-up guy. Instead, all he could think of was how badly he'd love to plant his fist in Marcus's face. The more rational part knew that was petty, and unfair. But he didn't really care. The man had walked in and taken everything from Brooks. But that wasn't fair, either. You couldn't take something you never had to start with. And like it or not, that was Marcus's daughter in there.

Not his.

How the hell was he supposed to live with Marcus

throwing that in his face for the rest of their lives? How was he supposed to deal with Marcus *period* for the rest of their lives? The best part of Marcus stealing their app idea was that he'd disappeared. He'd screwed Brooks and Cole over, but then he'd left. They hadn't had to deal with the weasel anymore. And now he'd have to deal with Marcus…forever.

The really shit part was that Marcus wasn't a total dickwad. At least when it came to Leah and the baby, which was a good thing. Marcus seemed like he knew what he was doing. Hell, having insurance had never even occurred to Brooks. If he got sick, he just called a doctor friend he knew and got it taken care of. But babies had to go to doctors for all kinds of things. Shots and stuff. And checkups. He knew nothing about babies. She'd been in his house not even a week and Brooks was sure she was already scarred for life. He didn't want that kind of responsibility. Everything would change. He'd need a new place, for sure, and he didn't want one. He liked his apartment. He liked his life.

Leah…

Brooks shut that down immediately. Dwelling on her and whatever idiotic fantasies he might have briefly entertained did no one any good. He was an irresponsible asshole and always would be. She and the baby were both better off with a guy like Marcus, no matter how irritating the guy was. Hell, he'd probably treat them both like queens every day of their lives just to prove to everyone he was a better guy than Brooks.

Brooks, on the other hand, might make everyone laugh for a few minutes, but no one went to him with serious problems. He wasn't the guy you turned to when shit hit the fan. He was the guy throwing the shit at the blades in the first place. He had no business around a new mother and an innocent baby.

It probably would have been better for them all if he'd

kept driving when he'd left the hospital that night. But there was no way he could have just left her there. So he'd gone back. And brought them home. Because there was really nothing else he could do at that moment. And maybe he wanted to steal a few final days with her. With them. But he knew it couldn't last.

It's what they'd planned to do from the start anyway. Things may have gotten a little muddled over the last few months, but neither of them had ever intended to stay together. And now with Marcus in the picture, it would be better for everyone if Brooks bowed out gracefully. And it should be easy. Bowing out was what he did.

He took a minute to compose himself. No one had ever seen through him the way Leah did. He didn't want her reading anything that wasn't there. Or shouldn't be there. Wouldn't be there once he got his life back.

Finally, he took a deep breath and opened the door.

Leah glanced up. When she saw him, her eyes lit up and for a second he savored that sweet addicting warmth that always flowed through him when they were together. She finished laying the baby in her bassinet and then sat back on the couch, one leg tucked under the other.

"Hey," he said.

"Hey." She took a deep breath. "Do you think you and Marcus will ever get along?"

Brooks straightened, stung that the first words out of her mouth would be about the other man. "Yeah, that's what we need to talk about. I don't think that's ever going to happen."

She raised an eyebrow. "Why? What happened with you guys before…that's all in the past, isn't it? Marcus is a good guy."

Brooks swallowed hard. "Yes, he is. When he's not around me. We don't bring out the best in each other."

She snorted. "I've noticed."

He rubbed his hand over his face. "Look, I know this whole thing is one big complicated mess. But Marcus is here and seems to be planning on staying and he *is* the baby's father." Saying those words was like spitting out acid, but it didn't change the truth of them. "Seems to me like we've got one extra person in the mix here. I think you've got your job at the school pretty secure now. They love you, and we'd always said that I traveled a lot so I don't think they'll notice if I'm not there. And with Marcus and I having issues that don't seem like they are going to be resolved anytime soon…"

Her eyes looked a bit brighter but if she was on the verge of tears, she thankfully held it together. "So what?" she asked. "Now that he's here you're going to bail?"

"Bail on what, Leah? Our fake marriage that wasn't supposed to last more than a few months? Isn't it time we both got back to our real lives? I know staying with me wasn't something you were planning on. Do you want to be tied to some irresponsible idiot for the rest of your life because I couldn't keep my mouth shut around your boss?"

"You're not an irresponsible idiot, Brooks. I mean, yes, you have your moments, like this one. But there is more to you than that."

"Not really."

"Oh, come on, Brooks. At least give me the real reason you're doing this."

"That is the real reason. I care about you, Leah. A lot. And I care about the baby. And you deserve a hell of a lot better than what I can give you. And I'm sorry, but there's no way I can deal with Marcus being in my face trying to get under my skin day in and day out. He'll drive me insane. We're already barely speaking and the baby is only a week old. What kind of environment is that to raise a kid in?"

"Can't you just let bygones be bygones and move on?"

"It's not that easy, Leah. It's kind of hard to let bygones

be bygones when the same shit keeps happening. I didn't plan on anything ever happening between us, and I'm sorry if that makes all this harder. But I really am trying to do what's best for everyone. I can't give you what you need."

"You don't know what I need. You've never even asked me."

"You've never asked me, either."

She looked like she was going to argue that point, but then dropped her gaze. The fact that he was hurting her tore him apart. But it was for the best. She'd see that eventually.

"I'm no good in relationships. The fact that I've never been in one long term should have been a good clue."

"That's just an excuse."

He shook his head. "You don't have to believe me. But I am doing what's best for everyone. You deserve better than me. And so does she," he said, nodding at the baby. "And I deserve a life where I don't have to constantly deal with someone who tries his hardest to undermine everything I do. Can you imagine me being the stepfather to his child? How is that ever going to work?"

She folded her arms and looked down at her feet. "It won't."

He paused for a few seconds, trying to force out the rest of it, reminding himself that this was what was best for her. Best for the baby. Best for him. Hell, even best for Marcus. They'd *all* be happier if he was out of the picture.

"I have to leave for a few weeks," he said.

"What?"

Her eyes grew wide with what looked like unshed tears. The sudden urge to drop to his knees and beg her to choose him washed over him and he choked it back. That wasn't in anyone's best interest. Marcus was an ass to Brooks, but in general, he was a stand-up guy, as much as Brooks hated to admit it. And he was the baby's real father. He was someone they could both depend on. Not a screwup goofball that people only kept around for laughs.

"There's a conference in Vienna. Cole doesn't want to travel yet with Piper being so small. One of us needs to go. I had planned on going anyway. Our…your baby wasn't supposed to be here for a few more weeks so I thought I had time. And…Marcus will be here if you need anything."

"I don't need anything. We'll do just fine on our own," she said, her voice hard as steel.

He kept going, not meeting her eyes. "I'm not sure how long I'll be gone. You can stay in the apartment for as long as you want. I have an account set up for you at the bank. All the information for it is in the top drawer of my desk. I've made sure you'll be comfortable."

She shook her head. "I don't want anything from you."

He clasped his hands behind his back, one hand grasping the other wrist so hard his fingers went numb. "Be that as it may, the money is there for you both if you need it. Don't be stubborn about it."

She just raised her chin in the air. "Is that all?"

He stared at her for a moment, his resolve wavering. All it would take from her was one word. If she asked him to stay… said to hell with Marcus, she wanted him…maybe they could work it out…

But she said nothing. So he nodded.

"Then go," she said, her voice barely audible.

He took a step back, but stopped, unable to make himself leave. "Leah…"

"Go!" she yelled, startling him and the baby who began to wail.

He didn't wait for her to tell him again. He'd made his choice. He turned on his heel and walked away from his only chance at happiness.

# Chapter Twenty-Three

Leah slid the last few books onto the shelf and then slumped onto the couch next to Kiersten who was busy cuddling the baby.

"Little Livy," Kiersten cooed to her, before smiling up at Leah. "How did you come up with Olivia?" she asked.

Leah kissed her baby's head. "Olivia was my grandmother's name. It seemed to suit my little princess."

"It certainly does. A beautiful name for a beautiful baby. It's perfect." Kiersten smiled again and then settled the baby back in her swing.

Leah laid her head back on the pillows with a sigh.

"So what do you think?" she asked, looking around the apartment.

"It's cute," Kiersten said.

"But?"

"But nothing."

Leah kept staring at her until Kiersten gave up. "Okay, if you must know, I guess I don't understand why you didn't stay at the apartment."

"At Brooks's apartment."

"He said you could stay there for as long as you wanted."

Leah shook her head. "I didn't feel comfortable there anymore. I wasn't all that comfortable to begin with, but at least before I had sort of a reason to be there. Now… We aren't together now. I shouldn't be staying in his apartment."

Kiersten frowned. "Have you heard from him?"

"No," Leah said, trying not to let her disappointment show. "He said he would be gone for a few weeks."

Kiersten sighed. "You guys were so good together."

"Apparently he didn't think so."

"I know he did. Maybe he's just afraid. It's a big step for a guy like him."

"It's a big step for anyone. I was afraid. I was angry. He was the one who walked away."

"Maybe if you tried talking to him again…"

Leah shook her head before Kiersten had even finished. "There's nothing to talk about. He made a lot of good points. The marriage was supposed to be temporary. We both got out of it what we needed. End of story. Now I need to start building a life for me and the baby. And he made it quite clear that he didn't want to be a part of that life."

Kiersten looked like she wanted to argue some more but thankfully she thought better of it. "So what about the other one?"

"Marcus?"

"Yes. Has he been around much?"

"He was at first, but he has a lot of things going on with his job. He still calls every day and tries to stop by every few days to see the baby. He always brings her a little present or something."

"That's sweet."

"Yeah. He's not a big help with the actual baby care stuff. And I hate to admit it, but listening to the way he talks about Brooks…Brooks was right. He and Marcus will never get along and I'm not raising my baby around two grown-ass men who can't be in the same room together. And Marcus is her father so if one of them isn't going to be in the picture…it kind of narrows the choices down."

"Well that sucks."

Leah sighed. "Yes, it does. Although maybe it won't matter anyway. Marcus is based in Hong Kong. He said he was going to transfer to New York, but I don't know how much he really wants that. All he talks about lately is going back."

Kiersten looked around the small apartment. "So, it's just going to be the two of you here alone?"

"It won't be so bad. I like it here. It's quiet and peaceful. And I kind of like the idea of being surrounded by nuns. No men to complicate things. Plus, the sisters love the baby. I'll never have to worry about finding a sitter."

"And the headmistress, Reverend Mother, whoever, is okay with the whole single mother thing?"

"Well, she doesn't really know about that part yet. We had always told her that Brooks traveled a lot. That's why she thinks I've moved back here, so I won't be alone in that big apartment with just me and the baby. Living here is easier for me to get back and forth to class and we're in a nice safe environment. Plus, the daycare is on campus and there's a preschool when Olivia gets older. It works perfectly. Once the divorce is final I will sit down and talk with Reverend Mother about everything."

Leah glanced over at the coffee table where her newly drawn-up divorce papers waited in a manila envelope. She hadn't signed them yet, hadn't even read them. They had the prenup. Neither one of them would profit from the marriage. Brooks had set up that bank account for her, but she hadn't touched it. And had no plans to.

Marcus came from old money, as he liked to remind everyone. Olivia would never want for anything. In fact, he'd been a little peeved that Leah still wanted to work. He could just join Brooks in that corner. She liked teaching. But he'd still insisted on setting up accounts for her and Livy. At least if she did use those accounts, it would be Marcus caring for his own child. Brooks had no ties to either of them. It wouldn't be right to use his money.

She had a good job with free living quarters and she could eat at the cafeteria whenever she wanted. She would be able to provide a nice life for Livy without Brooks's help.

"When are you going to send him the papers?" Kiersten asked.

"I don't know. Tomorrow I guess. Better to get it over with."

"Leah, you really don't have to do this."

"Yes, I do." She took a deep breath and slowly blew it out. "I'm still angry with him for walking out on us. But I can't really blame him. We aren't his responsibility. We never were. He never made any promises. And he never made any secret of the fact that he never wanted to be a husband or father. He might have gotten caught up in the whole baby thing while it was happening, but thankfully we came to our senses before it was too late. Before Livy was older and had grown attached. It's better this way. He doesn't need a wife and a baby cramping his style. And with Marcus in the mix making him miserable…" She sighed. "I get it. Marcus does seem to enjoy needling him. Co-parenting with those two would be a nightmare. Now Brooks can get back to living his life the way he likes it."

"Are you sure that's how he still wants it? Because I'll tell you what, I've known Brooks for several years now, and I've never seen him even remotely as happy as he was with you."

A little spark of hope flared in Leah's heart, but she

extinguished it immediately. "If that was really true he wouldn't have walked out on us. He left me sitting in *his* apartment and I haven't seen or heard from him since."

"But you love him, don't you?"

Leah's gaze shot to Kiersten's. "That doesn't make any difference."

"Of course it does," Kiersten said. "You need to tell him."

"Why? So he can reject me all over again? So I can watch him walk out the door again? I've already gone through that once. I have no intention of doing it again. He made his choice clear when he left us a week after Livy was born. We don't have any place in his world. I never fit in with his crowd. Even if he thinks he wants us now, he'll change his mind eventually. The last thing he needs or wants is full-time responsibility for a child who isn't his for the next two decades, especially with Marcus there every step of the way." She shook her head. "I'll sign the papers tonight and send them tomorrow. Then we can both move on with our lives."

Kiersten looked at her sadly. "I hope you're making the right decision."

"So do I," she said.

Either way, there was no turning back now.

• • •

Brooks sat in his office, the divorce papers spread out on his desk in front of him. He hadn't thought she'd send them so soon. And the fact that she had only proved that he had been right in leaving when he did. There wasn't much there to read. They had a pretty ironclad prenup, though he didn't like the terms. He would feel much better if she would take alimony or at least a nice settlement. He'd set up the bank account for her but he knew she hadn't touched it yet. Knew she would never touch it. He slammed the pen down on his desk. Stubborn woman. But if that's the way she wanted it then fine. He picked up his pen and signed the papers quickly before he could change his mind.

"You're an idiot, mate."

Brooks glanced up to see Harrison standing in his door way.

"Well, that's certainly not the first time you've said that to me."

"No, but it might be the one time you've deserved it the most. How do you have a woman like that and then just walk away from her?"

Brooks scowled at him. "I don't have her. I never had her. And the woman sent me divorce papers. Exactly what else am I supposed to do with those?"

Harrison shrugged. "I don't know. Shred them. Burn them. Fold them up into little hearts and write a million apology notes on them. Anything would be better than signing them."

"Too late for that," Brooks said. "They're already signed."

"Well then, you deserve every year of miserable lonely life left to you."

Brooks stared at him, shock coursing through him at the stark, depressing sentiment. "You really suck at cheering up a friend when he's down."

"That's not why I came here. You don't deserve to be cheered up. I was hoping to knock some sense into you."

"About what? You're acting like I had a choice in this matter."

"Didn't you? No one forced you to walk away and no one certainly forced you to sign those damn papers. That was all you."

"I did it for her."

"Why? Because she's better off without you? Don't give me that load of bollocks. You didn't walk away because it was better for her; you did it because it was easier for you. It's easier to say that she's better off without you than to try and win her heart and fail. This way you still get to play the hero who is sacrificing his own happiness for the woman he loves. When in reality you're too busy wallowing to go fight for her."

"There's no point in fighting. Marcus is there. She doesn't need me."

"First of all, stop using Marcus as an excuse. She barely knows the man, and doesn't seem to have any desire to get to know him better except for the sake of her daughter, and more importantly the man is based out of the country. He's not here for longer than a few weeks at a time anyway, and from what I heard he has no plans to change that. So saying you're staying away so that he can be with her is about the dumbest excuse I've ever heard. Second of all, of course she doesn't need you. She's a strong, independent woman. She doesn't need anybody. That doesn't mean she doesn't want you. And that's not the question you should be asking yourself anyway. The real question is, do you need her?"

Brooks sat quietly for a moment, Harrison's words soaking into his brain. "Yes, I need her. Not being with her physically hurts," he said finally.

"Well, then…"

"But it doesn't matter. The last time I saw her she screamed at me to get out. She doesn't want anything to do with me."

"You pissed her off, mate. Been known to happen. Then again, women have been known to change their minds on occasion, too. But you have to give them a reason to. You haven't told her anything except that you're not good enough, you're not right for her, you can't deal with the one man she can't cut out of her life. So why don't you start showing her that you were wrong. You keep saying she made her choice, but you never gave her any other choice to make."

Damn. He hated it when Harrison made sense. "Okay, then. If I concede that you have a valid point?"

"Then I guess you need to decide what you're going to do about it."

Brooks shook his head. "I'm never going to deserve her, you know."

"You going to let that stop you?"

Brooks grabbed the papers off his desk.

"What are you going to do?" Harrison asked.

Brooks met his gaze and stood, the papers crumpling in his hand. "Go see Marcus, first of all. After that…I have no fucking clue. Guess I'll just have to make shit up as I go along."

# Chapter Twenty-Four

Leah handed Marcus the diaper bag and the little cooler that had baggies of her breast milk. "You sure you'll be okay?" she asked him for the thirtieth time.

He laughed. "I promise, we'll be fine. It'll be good to spend some time with my little princess before I head back to Hong Kong. And my mom will be with us the whole time. She won't let me screw anything up too badly. And you'll only be a phone call away if I need you."

Leah nodded. "Seriously, if you need me, I can be there in a flash. Just call. Even if it's for something small. You never know..."

"Leah, we'll be okay. Now go have fun with your friend. Spend a few baby-free hours relaxing."

She nodded. She knew she was being silly, but it was also her first time away from Olivia. Marcus generally came to visit at her apartment, but he was heading back to Hong Kong soon and wanted to spend a few hours with the baby, show her off to some extended family who was in town. Leah would have gone also, but Kiersten insisted on whisking her away for a spa day. Which, honestly, did sound heavenly. So Leah agreed to let Marcus take Livy for a few hours. She'd known it would be hard. She hadn't known it would be like ripping out a piece of her soul and letting him take it for a spin around the block.

Moments after Marcus pulled away, a town car with tinted windows pulled up.

Only it wasn't Kiersten who climbed out of the backseat.

Her heart stopped for a second before doing the butterfly dance with her stomach. "Brooks? What are you doing here? I thought Kiersten was supposed to…"

"I bribed her into setting up the date with you. Don't get mad," he said at her frown. "I needed to talk to you, and you didn't seem inclined to give me the time any other way."

"You could have just asked, you know."

"Yeah, but where's the fun in that?"

She started smiling in spite of herself. How did he always get her to do that? Her phone buzzed and she pulled it out of her pocket. A text from Kiersten.

*Don't be mad! He promised free babysitting for a month. Can't pass that up. Hear him out okay.*

She glanced back up at him. He stood at the open door of the car with such a hopeful expression she couldn't bring herself to say no.

"What is all this about?"

He stepped back from the door and gestured for her to get inside. "If you'll come with me…"

She raised her eyebrows, not sure she wanted to go down this whole road with him again. He still hadn't sent in the divorce papers. Which surprised her, considering he was the one who walked out in the first place.

"Brooks…"

"Please," he said. "I know I was an unforgiveable ass, but

we've already established what an idiot I am. Just…please. One hour."

She sighed. This was probably a really bad idea, but she couldn't say no to him. "Fine. One hour."

The big grin he flashed her had her heart skipping through her chest like a little girl with a lollipop. She climbed in the car and he slid in next to her. They didn't talk much until she noticed they were heading out of the city.

"Brooks, where are we going? I need to be home by four. Marcus is bringing the baby back."

"I know, don't worry. I'll have you back in time."

"What do you mean you know?"

"I spoke with Marcus this morning."

"You what?"

"We sat down and had a nice, long talk. And both walked out without a single drop of blood being shed. You should be proud. Now, just be patient for once," he said with a grin. "I have a surprise set up for you."

"A surprise, huh? Am I going to like it?"

For a moment the excitement in his eyes dulled. "I really don't know. But I hope so."

They didn't say anything else but the silence wasn't uncomfortable. He was one of the only people she could sit in a room with without saying a word and not feel the need to fill the silence. When they started winding through neighborhoods of large family homes she sat forward, watching out the window.

"Where are we?"

"We're almost there," he said, the excitement back in his voice.

They finally pulled into a quiet, tree-lined cul-de-sac, lined with beautiful two- and three-story homes. They came to a stop in front of the house at the back of the cul-de-sac. A picture-perfect white house with black shutters and a flower box beneath each window. There were several blossoming trees in the yard and a flower-lined path up to the front door.

And a white picket fence. It had an actual white picket fence.

"Brooks," she said with a tremor in her voice, beginning to have an inkling of what this might be about.

"Come on," he said, opening the door and sliding out. He held out a hand to help her from the car.

"Whose house is this?" she asked.

Brooks still held her hand. He pulled her to his side, wrapping an arm around her waist. "It's yours, if you want it."

"What?" she said, her voice barely more than a whisper.

"Come on," he said, tugging at her hand like a little kid in a candy store. "Let me show you the rest."

He almost dragged her into the house as she tried to catch a glimpse of every corner of the home she had always dreamed of.

Inside was as perfect as she'd always envisioned. Hardwood floors, a light airy spacious kitchen, a family room with a fireplace—she could already picture spending nights watching movies before a roaring fire with the baby and… maybe…

"I haven't showed you the best part yet," he said, pulling her toward another room.

He opened a set of French doors and her heart just about stopped.

"Oh, Brooks," she said, choking back the lump that formed in her throat.

He led her into a room, a library really. With wall-to-wall built-in shelves just waiting for books. There was a fireplace in this room as well, and a big bay window with a window seat.

"My own library?" she asked, suddenly feeling like Belle in *Beauty and the Beast*. It took everything she had not to jump on the ladders and start singing while rolling along the shelves.

Brooks rested a hand on one of the rolling ladders. "Do you like it?"

"Do I like it? Brooks, this is just… It's incredible."

He beamed. "I have one more thing to show you," he said, pulling her out of the library and toward another set of French doors that led outside. He opened them and drew her onto a deck that overlooked the large backyard. On one side, someone had planted a garden where she could already see neat rows of vegetables and herbs beginning to sprout. The rest of the yard looked like it was right out of *Better Homes and Gardens* with neatly manicured lawns overflowing with flowers and trees. And on the other side of the yard was a swing set and playhouse just waiting to be used.

She sat on the steps of the deck and raised a shaking hand to her mouth as she looked around the yard she had always wanted.

"Do you like it?" Brooks asked her again.

"I've never seen anything more beautiful in my life. This is…perfect."

He flashed that huge smile again and sat a couple steps below her. "I'm so glad you like it. It's in a really good school district, too. One of the top-ranked districts. The elementary school is only two blocks away so you could walk Olivia to school every day if you wanted. And there's a dance studio about a ten-minute drive from here where they teach all kinds of classes. They even do piano lessons there if that's something she's interested in. The community center isn't too far away either and there's a big library about three miles down the road that way," he said, pointing behind him. "And I checked the crime databanks. This is one of the safest neighborhoods in the city. Most of the people here don't even lock their doors when they leave."

"You actually checked on all of that stuff?"

He looked at her a little surprised. "I went and visited each place. I even met the kindergarten teacher, though I know it's a little early for that yet. But I wanted to make sure it would be a good place for Olivia to grow up. Oh and..." He shoved his hand in his pocket and for a second Leah's heart stopped. But, instead of the ring she thought he might be pulling out, he handed her a key.

"What's this for?" she asked.

"You'll need to be able to get Olivia to school and her dance and piano classes. And if you want to go into the city you'll definitely need something to drive."

She sucked in a breath. "You bought me a car?"

"A minivan," he said with a huge grin. "It's actually a pretty sweet ride. I drove it sixty miles and never felt a bump. Seriously, it's the quietest car I've ever been in. It's top of the line, complete with a DVD system, which the guy at the dealership told me is popular with kids. I know you don't need something that big just yet, but the dealership guy said that they are good for things like carpools. And if you ever decided to have more kids..."

She didn't know what to think. He was quite literally handing her everything she had always wanted. Well, almost everything.

"And you're giving this all to me?"

He nodded. "No strings attached. If you want it, this is all yours. But I will admit I had hoped..."

He pulled a stick figure of a man out of his back pocket. One of those kinds that people put on the back window of their car to represent everyone in the family.

"Yours and Olivia's are already on the car. I hoped... maybe..." He took a deep breath and then took her hands in his. "I know I screwed up, Leah. Really, seriously screwed up. My only excuse is that I thought I was doing what was best for you and the baby. I didn't think I was what you needed. You deserve far better than me. And, honestly, I was terrified. And an idiot. And I've never regretted anything more in my life. What I was too stubborn to realize is that I'm the one who needs you. Who still needs you. Who will always need you. I know I don't deserve you. I don't deserve another chance. But…"

"What about Marcus? He's not going away, Brooks. He's Livy's father…"

"I know. And for her sake, we're going to work on getting along. He…"

His face flushed and he pulled up his calendar on his phone, showing it to her. She glanced down and gasped out a surprised laugh. "You two are going to couples counseling?"

He let out a long-suffering sigh. "Remote sessions on the video conference line. His idea. But…it's not a bad one. We're both determined to get along."

She smiled at him, her heart overflowing. "That's an excellent start."

He took her hands again. "I know you don't need me but…"

Leah reached out and put a finger against his lips. "You're wrong." She cupped his cheek. "I do need you. This place," she said, gesturing around her to encompass the house. "It's amazing, incredible. Everything I always dreamed. But the dream wouldn't be complete without you here."

Brooks stood and pulled her into his arms. "Will you marry me? Again? For real this time?"

Leah laughed. "I would be honored to be your wife. For real."

His smile lit a fire in her that would burn until the day she died.

He put his hand in his pocket again and she laughed. "How much do you have stashed in there?"

"This is the last thing."

This time he pulled out a small velvet box. He opened it to reveal a tastefully beautiful ring, the stones arranged in the shape of a flower. Big enough to be impressive, but not so big that she'd be embarrassed to wear it.

"I knew you wouldn't want anything too big…" he said, his uncertainty chipping away at her heart. "The first one I picked out was twice this size. And I had the jeweler put it on hold just in case. But I know when we talked about it before with the wedding bands you were ridiculously stubborn about it…"

She laughed and leaned forward to kiss him. "It's absolutely perfect, Brooks. I've never seen anything more beautiful."

He slipped the ring on her finger and kissed her, long and deep, searing the moment in her heart forever.

Then he broke away, laughing, and swept her into his arms.

"Come on," he said. "Let's go christen the bedroom."

# Epilogue

Olivia Brooke Cassidy, named to honor both her fathers, was christened in the tiny stone church on the banks of the Greek island where Piper Harrington had been christened a year before. The party had continued into the wee hours of the morning, though Leah and Brooks had escorted the guest of honor back to the yacht not too long after the ceremony. Little ones needed to be in bed at a proper time.

And it was her parents' honeymoon after all.

A strange one, maybe. Leah was sure most couples didn't take all their closest friends with them on their honeymoons. But they'd wanted to go back to where they'd first met. And it seemed a good idea to start a new tradition with the christenings. Well, a second tradition. They had another one going with the prenups. Brooks had insisted they sign Kiersten's version the second time around. Well, the preliminary version that simply stated that anything she says goes. Kiersten keeps adding to it. Leah protested, but Brooks wouldn't take no for an answer. Stubborn fool.

The christenings were a tradition Leah was much happier

to follow. Now with Cole and Kiersten's baby and Leah and Brooks's baby newly christened at the little church, it felt well on its way. Especially since there might be another little one to be christened before too long.

Leah handed Kiersten a towel and a glass of ice water with mint leaves.

"Thanks," Kiersten said gratefully, sipping on the cool water. "I don't know why I'm getting seasick this time. I've always done fine before."

Leah raised an eyebrow. "Unless you're not seasick this time. You could be pregnant."

Kiersten's eyes widened. "Oh God."

Leah laughed. "You might want to get that checked when we get home."

Kiersten nodded. Then she laughed, too. "Well, I did want to have more kids. I was planning on putting a little more space between them. But I'll hold off the panicking until I find out for sure."

The ladies settled against the chaise longues and sipped on their drinks, waving as their men occasionally sped by the boat on their jet skis. A particularly rambunctious round of laughter drew their attention to where Brooks bobbed up and down in the water. Marcus reached out a hand and helped drag him back over to his jet ski, both men laughing and slapping each other's backs.

"So how's that all working out?" Kiersten asked, nodding at the two of them.

"Pretty well, actually."

"Brooks was okay with you giving Livy Marcus's last name?"

"Surprisingly, yes. Though he couldn't really argue that one."

"When is Marcus leaving again?"

"Next week. His new Hong Kong office opens soon so

he'll be gone for a while this time. We'll keep him updated, send pictures, that kind of thing. And he'll get visitation when he's in town. He wants to know her, and be a part of her life. But with his job… It's easier for us to have full custody. He's going to stay based in Hong Kong, permanently."

"Yikes."

"And he signed papers giving Brooks guardianship if anything happens to both of us. None of us wanted there to be any problem with him maintaining custody if something ever happened. And since we don't need child support or anything like that he's going to set aside money every month into a college fund for Livy. He wants to be able to contribute to her life in some way."

"He sounds like a really great guy."

Leah nodded again. "Livy is lucky to have two such amazing dads."

"Yes she is," Kiersten said. "Now you just need to get started on giving her some siblings."

Leah laughed. "I'd love nothing more. Though I'd prefer to have Livy out of diapers first."

Kiersten snorted. "Amen."

Leah excused herself for a minute. The men had brought the jet skis in a few minutes before but Brooks hadn't reappeared yet. She wandered to the back of the boat and stopped short at the sight that met her eyes. Brooks sat on the deck cross-legged with the baby in his lap. He was pointing out the various interesting things on the shoreline. The baby didn't know what he was pointing out of course. But she gurgled contentedly, waving her little fists as he spoke to her. Brooks looked up and saw her watching them and beckoned her over with a smile. She sat down beside him, leaning in for a kiss.

"Sorry," she said. "I didn't want to interrupt. But you two looked like you were having so much fun, I couldn't resist."

He kissed her again. "Joining in the party, huh? What happened to my strict schoolteacher? I thought marriage wasn't supposed to be fun."

"Maybe you've changed my mind. I don't think marriage to you could be anything but fun."

"And that's a good thing?"

She kissed his cheek and wrapped her arms around him, cuddling into him. "Absolutely. I'm serious enough for the both of us. I definitely needed some fun in my life."

"I'm happy I can be of service."

She laughed and kissed his shoulder before reaching out to take Livy's little hand.

"And by the way," Brooks said, resting his cheek against her head, "you are never an interruption. I'm always happiest when I have both my girls at my side."

"Then I guess it's a good thing you'll always have us."

He wrapped his arm around her waist to draw her closer. "A very, very good thing."

# Acknowledgments

As always, my deepest thanks to my dream team at Entangled. Alethea Spiridon, editing goddess extraordinaire, I really couldn't do this without you! Thank you for your never ending support, amazing insight, tireless work, and kind replies to my stress-induced emails. Many massive thanks also to Riki Cleveland and Jessica Turner, my incredible publicity team, without whom I'd be standing on corners begging people to buy my books. Thank you so much for everything you do to get my books out in the world!

To my sweet husband and amazing kids. You are my everything. Always. To my sweet family—thank you for being my biggest cheerleaders. I can't tell you what it means to know I always have you in my corner. I love you all!

To Toni, for always being in my corner and always being there for me. And to Sarah Ballance, my writing creepy twin—I'm not sure what's going on with our mouse invasion lately but the fact that we seem to be having the same invasion from a thousand miles apart might be taking our whole creepy twin thing to an unhealthy level. Then again, that seems to completely works for us. So, may the non-mice factions prevail!

# About the Author

Kira Archer resides in Pennsylvania with her husband, two kiddos, and far too many animals in the house. She tends to laugh at inappropriate moments and break all the rules she gives her kids (but only when they aren't looking), and would rather be reading a book than doing almost anything else. She has odd, eclectic tastes in just about everything and often lets her imagination run away with her. She loves her romances a little playful, a lot sexy, and always with a happily ever after. She also writes historical romances as Michelle McLean.

***Discover the* Winning the Billionaire *series…***

69 MILLION THINGS I HATE ABOUT YOU

***Also by Kira Archer***

PRETENDING WITH THE GREEK BILLIONAIRE

DRIVING HER CRAZY

KISSING HER CRAZY

LOVING HER CRAZY

TRULY, MADLY, SWEETLY

TOTALLY, SWEETLY, IRREVOCABLY

SWEETLY, DEEPLY, ABSOLUTELY

***Discover more category romance titles from Entangled Indulgence...***

## Besting the Billionaire

a *Billionaire Bad Boys* novel by Alison Aimes

Billionaire Alexander Kazankov and Lily Bennett go toe-to-toe in an ugly, take no prisoners battle to prove they're the right choice to be CEO of the same company. All too soon playing dirty in the boardroom leads to playing even dirtier in the dark. It's destined to end in personal and professional disaster. So why the hell can't they stop?

## The Baby Project

a *Kingston Family* novel by Miranda Liasson

Liz Kingston spends her life delivering babies and longs for one of her own. Who better to ask than her sexy ex-fling, who has no interest in ever settling down or being a father. Nothing in all of international correspondent Grant Wilbanks's experience could have prepared him for the way a torrid affair with Liz makes him feel. When she asks for his assistance, he figures he can help her out with a simple donation. No strings, no emotions, just... test-tube science. But this simple favor gives them both more than they ever bargained for.

## The Billionaire's Bet

a *Sexy Billionaires* novel by Victoria Davies

Caleb Langston wants one thing. Revenge. Hailey Mitchel is his ticket to finally evening the score with his old adversary. There's just one problem. The more time he spends with her, the less he cares about his grand plans for payback. But love is always a gamble, and soon he'll have to choose between his past and his future. And pray Hailey never discovers the secret he's been hiding from her.

## The Irredeemable Billionaire

a *Muse* novel by Lexxie Couper

It seems fate is playing with Sebastian when he's given community service and the boy he's assigned in the Big Brother program turns out to be the son of the one person he's never been able to charm. Grace has her hands full. The last thing she needs is for the bane of her teenage existence to show up. Even worse is the fact that she's no longer immune to his devastating smile and sexy eyes.

Made in the USA
San Bernardino, CA
15 March 2018